Contents

Foreword i

Introduction iii

1. Intimacy, Intercession, and Increase 1

Part 1: INTIMACY 4

2. Knowing God 5

3. Knowing God as Father: Jesus 8

4. Knowing God as Father: Us 11

5. Knowing Jesus as Friend 16

6. Knowing the Holy Spirit 19

7. A Two-Way Conversation 22

8. Tuning into God's Voice 28

9. Is That You, God? 32

10. Are You a Trustworthy Friend? 38

Part 2: INTERCESSION 46

11. Intercession: a Get-To 47

12. What's in the Power of a Name? 50

13. First of All... 53

14. Persistent Prayer 58

15. Prayer of the Righteous 62

16. You've Got to Have Faith 65

17. Corporate Prayer: Agreement 68

18. Do You Need to Say Amen? 72

19. Prophetic Prayer 77

Foreword

You are invited! Yes, you are invited to become a fellow traveler on a road trip. This journey will take you to new places, to exciting mountain peaks, to incredible views, to pristine valleys. You will not be the same at the end of this adventure!

In the 1970s, I was in my teens and part of a wonderful Christian youth group. We would get together with young people from all across North America and have car rallies. These would be two- or three-hour races through a city or across the country with check-ins, things to find, and some tough spots. Timing was critical. It was a race. Such an event would never happen today for safety reasons, but back then, before seatbelts were mandatory and before airbags existed, we would race from point to point just trying to get through the rally as quickly as possible. In each car we would have a driver, a navigator who had a big paper map spread out on his or her lap, and possibly one or two riders in the back seat. It was lots of fun, good fellowship, and very dangerous! The whole goal was to get through it as quickly as possible to get to the finish line.

This is not a car rally! The adventure Lyndal is inviting you on here is entirely different. I have personally taken this journey, each day of it. I can assure you that it is a great adventure and stretching, but the way to win is not with speed. You lose if you go fast. The way to win is to slow down and enjoy each leg of the journey.

I am reminded of the soul-searching verse in Psalm 27:8 where the psalmist has heard the Lord say "Come and talk with me." He responds, "LORD, I am coming" (NLT). How many times in my childhood did my mother ask me to do something to which I responded "Coming!" but then I continued with whatever I was doing? It used to drive my mother crazy, and I think my wife feels the same way sometimes!

God beckons you on this journey because He wants to spend time with you. He wants to take you to new places. He loves you, and He wants your company. Get up and start! Don't answer "Lord, I'm coming" and then stay where you are. God bless you on this journey, and stay safe!

—Dave Brereton, International Director, YFCI

Introduction

This devotional has one aim—to encourage a greater life of prayer in the reader. It can be used as an introduction to prayer for those who are new believers or a refresher for those who have been walking with the Lord for a longer period of time, but the primary audience it's written for is youth and young adults who desire to grow in this area. I draw upon personal experience and decades of work with young people to explore this vital topic. It is not a theological treatise, nor an exegetical study, yet at times it will ask the reader to think deeply about certain issues. It doesn't exhaust the topic of prayer by any means, but it gives a taste for further discovery.

The devotional is thirty-one days long so that it can be completed by reading one per day for a month. It is set out in three sections: intimacy (with God), intercession, and increase—with John 17 being a guiding passage. Within each day there are scriptures to read, thoughts to consider, reflections to ponder and action points to undertake.

Interwoven throughout are real-life stories that give testimony to the work of God and the power of prayer in people's lives. The desire is that these stories will inspire the reader to see what is possible through a life of prayer and obedience. As two Moravian missionaries said, as they departed by ship to the West Indies to preach to the slaves, "The Lamb who was slain is worthy to receive the reward of His suffering."[1]

Lyndal

God has given us His eternal life.

---

[1] Felicity Jensz, *German Moravian Missionaries in the British Colony of Victoria, Australia, 1848–1908: Influential Strangers.* (BRILL, 2010). PDF.

DAY 1

Intimacy, Intercession, and Increase

READ

John 17
I suggest reading it in two or three
versions, perhaps the ESV and also
The Passion Translation—for ease of
understanding.

Father, glorify Me in Your presence @ the glory I had with You
before the World began.
They knew for certainty that I came from You - they believed You sent me.
Protect them by the power of Your name - they may be one as we are one."
Sanctify them Father by the truth.   Unity!

1

Today we embark on a thirty-one-day adventure to learn more about prayer. But I don't want this to just be about gaining more head knowledge. I want you to be so excited and inspired by prayer that it becomes a part of your everyday life. Prayer is a verb. Yes, the dictionary says it's a noun, but in reality, it all comes down to the doing. So as we start, say a little prayer and ask God to show you what it is you need to learn and put into practice.

The adventure starts at John 17. Why this passage? Because it's one of the most beautiful recorded prayers of Jesus we have. In it, He models two of the most important aspects of prayer, which we will explore in more detail throughout these thirty-one days—intimacy with the Father and intercession. The third aspect we will investigate is the way prayer can be used in evangelism to increase the kingdom. This increase is suggested in John 17:20, where we see Jesus praying for those who would believe as a result of the words of His followers.

Now before you roll your eyes at another one of those Christian alliterations, just think about the meaning of these words and why they are so significant. These three words basically sum up the Christian life. Jesus died and rose again so we could have our sins wiped out, which enables us to live in an intimate relationship with God. He actually enters fully into us, so He gives us His heart for the world. We want to pray for the world and those in it. We want to see the kingdom of God increase throughout the world. Jesus commanded us to "go make disciples" (Matthew 28:19). What an exciting adventure we get to have as we give ourselves to these things!

Are you ready for the ride? Let's surrender to the driver, King Jesus, and say in our hearts, "Take us where You want us to go."

How have you viewed prayer up to this point in your life? Has it been an emergency escape, where you just shoot up a "help" to some being when you are in strife? Does it conjure up images of old people sitting around in a circle, praying very long prayers to an invisible God? Maybe you picture long lists of prayer requests or a long chain of beads and think *How boring.* Is it a have-to of the Christian life? I hope in the next thirty-one days, you'll discover the true meaning and delight of prayer.

Do you have a mentor or someone who is discipling you? This is someone you trust who you can share with, pray with and ask them to pray for you. If not, consider who you may ask to help you in your walk with Jesus. This could be a local youth pastor or youth leader, someone in a Youth for Christ center, or even a more mature family member who you look up to.

JOHN 17: 1-3 [Jewish leaders wanted to kill Jesus so He didn't want to go to Judah - went around in Galilee. Jewish Festival of Tabernacles was near - Jesus brothers said Leave Galilee & go to Judea - so that your brothers there may see the works you do.]

Part 1

INTIMACY

Ps. 63:1-8 Earnestly seek
Whole being thirst for You
Seen You in the sanctuary [Behold Your POWER/ GLORY]
Your love is better than LIFE
I praise/ lift up Your name - SATISFIED.
Remember You on my bed
You are my help - I sing,
I cling to You, My precious Heavenly Father
Your right hand upholds me DAILY!

4

Matt. 7:21-23   Only those who to the WILL OF THE FATHER
               will enter His Kingdom.

- WE PROPHESIED IN YOUR NAME   } I will profess to them
- CAST OUT DEMONS IN YOUR NAME } "I NEVER KNEW YOU!
- DONE WONDERFUL WORKS   } ↳ DEPART FROM ME,
                                 YOU WORK INIQUITY."

DAY
2

Knowing God

READ

Psalm 63:1-8 *PRAISING*
Matthew 7:21-23 *DO WILL OF FATHER - rejection*
John 17:1-3; 25-26 *KNOW GOD & JESUS CHRIST*
Philippians 3:10 *SHARE IN SUFFERINGS!*

I want to know Christ - YES, to know the
power of His ressurection & participation
in His sufferings, becoming like Him in
death.

John 17:1-3 Father the hour has come, Glorify Your Son, that
            Your Son might glorify You. You granted Him authority
            over all people - give eternal life to all You've given.
25-26   ETERNAL LIFE: they might know You... THE ONLY
            TRUE GOD & JESUS CHRIST.
I have made YOU known to them - ♡ you have for Me may be in them
& I may be in them

What do you think of when you think of the word "intimacy"? Does it freak you out? Does it give you the warm fuzzies? Does it make you think of things you know you shouldn't be thinking about? English is a funny language, with so many words having various meanings. Fortunately, the word intimacy doesn't have too many and we can narrow it down:

INTIMACY (noun) + close familiarity or friendship

The word intimacy isn't even in the Bible, so why use it? Because, I believe, it conveys a sense of closeness better than any other English word we have. The word the Bible uses is "know," which is a bit boring but packed with meaning if you dig a little deeper. The Greek word for intimacy is *ginosko*, which was used in John 17:3 and 17:25–27, and it is the same word that was used for an intimate relationship between a man and a woman (see Matthew 1:24–25 NKJV). Now that's pretty close.

Jesus says eternal life is to know the only true God and Jesus Christ. He even said people could be doing all this stuff for God but in the end it wouldn't count because He never knew them (Matthew 7:23). God desperately desires a close relationship with people, a relationship that begins now, here on earth, and that will last forever into eternity.

Do you really know God or do you just know about Him? There is a vast difference between having head knowledge about Him and having an intimate relationship with Him. Today, why don't you pray and say to God, "I truly want to know you." May this be the beginning of a deepening relationship with Him.

Take some time to make a list of the things you would like to get to know about God. How can you find out these things? You may like to come back to this list at a later date to see if you have found out the answers!

KNOW PERSONALLY · His salvation
& INTIMATELY   His deliverance
                 His freedom / saving power
                 His protection
                 His provision
                 His mercy / grace
                 His faithfulness

DAY 3

Knowing God as Father: Jesus

READ

This is my Son with whom I am well pleased.

TRANSFIGURATION - Peter, James, John

Matthew 3:17; 17:5 "This is my Son, whom I love, with Him I am well pleas."

Mark 14:36

John 17:1–26

Mk 14:36 ABBA FATHER, everything is possible for you. Take this cup from me. Yet not what I will, but what you will.

John 17:1-26 - Jesus prays to be Glorified.
Jesus prays for His Disciples - PROTECT THEM / KEEP THEM SAFE.
- MAY THEY BE ONE @ US.
- PROTECT THEM FROM THE EVIL ONE.
- SANCTIFY THEM @ YOUR TRUTH!

Righteous Father - they know You sent Me.
- I made You known. 8 So the LOVE You have for ME, will be to them & will continue in them.
to make You known.

Did you notice that in John 17, Jesus addresses God
as Father six times? In fact, if you read all the words
of Jesus in John's gospel (the red letters if you have
one of those Bibles), He mentions His Father no
fewer than *111 times.* Yes, I counted them all. That's
not to mention the other verses that *aren't* Jesus's
direct words. John is communicating a vital message
of the gospel—God is Father. Mark reveals Jesus
using the term *Abba* to pray to God. This was the
Aramaic word for father, which was used by children
to address their dads in the everyday life of Aramaic-
speaking people (which Jesus was). This shows God
is an accessible, close God who's concerned with our
everyday lives, not a distant God who is too busy
ruling the universe to have time for us.

Jesus was so sure of His position as a Son, a beloved
Son, that He knew He could call on His Father
anytime, whether it was in His deepest time of need
or to declare His praises (Matthew 11:25–26). He
truly knew the love and pleasure of His Father
(Matthew 3:17; 17:5). And it was important that
Jesus's followers really knew He was from the Father
and that they could also have the same kind of
intimate relationship with the Father as He did. The
love the Father had for Jesus could be *in* them (John
17:25–26). Wow. Now that is a game changer.

You may well be thinking, *No way could I have that
kind of relationship with God. After all, Jesus was
God's Son.* Well, before you follow that train of
thought for too long, just wait until tomorrow's
devotion and you'll find out just how beloved you
are.

What is your relationship with your earthly father
like? Is he close and accessible or distant and *COULD BE CLOSER .*
disinterested? Sometimes it is painful to think about
your own dad, but the way you view him can
sometimes impact the way you view God. Ask God
to show you if you believe some things about Him
that aren't true. *HARD TIMES - distant . - not compassionate*
- uncaring
- silent

Write down what you currently believe about what
kind of Father God is like. If you don't know, that's
ok. Pray - God, would you please show me what kind
of Father you are like as I take this journey with
Jesus?

I've asked for forgiveness & again today.
I realize the DARK, PAINFUL, CONFUSED & HURTING
heart clouded out the TRUTH that You are
ALWAYS present, caring, compassionate
regardless of my hurting, damaged emotions.
Forever grateful for sustaining, protecting, caring &
keeping a watchful (10) *eye on me.*
I adore You!

EPH. 1:4-6 CHOSE US BEFORE CREATION... TO BE HOLY & BLAMELESS IN HIS SIGHT. IN ♡ PREDESTINED US FOR ADOPTION TO SONSHIP → JESUS CHRIST, @ HIS PLEASURE & WILL - TO THE PRAISE OF HIS GLORIOUS PRAISE (GRACE) - WHICH HE FREELY GAVE US IN THE ONE HE ♡.

2:18 THROUGH HIS SON WE HAVE ACCESS TO THE FATHER → HIS SON.

JOHN 1:1
IN THE BEGINNING WAS THE WORD & THE WORD WAS @ GOD, & THE WORD WAS GOD.

DAY
4

Knowing God
as
Father: Us

JAMES 1:16-18
Don't be deceived brothers & sisters. EVERY GOOD & PERFECT GIFT COMES FROM ABOVE - THE FATHER HEAVENLY LIGHTS, WHO DOES NOT CHANGE LIKE SHIFTING SHADOWS. HE CHOSE TO GIVE US BIRTH → THE WORD OF TRUTH, SO THAT WE MIGHT BE A KIND OF FIRST FRUITS OF ALL HE CREATED.

READ

Matthew 6:9 YOUR FATHER KNOWS WHAT YOU NEED BEFORE YOU ASK. OUR FATHER, HALLOWED BE YOUR NAME
John 20:17 I AM ASCENDING TO MY FATHER & YOUR FATHER TO MY GOD & YOUR GOD.
Romans 8:15-17
Galatians 4:6 BECAUSE YOU ARE SONS, GOD SENT HIS SPIRIT SONS INTO OUR ♡s, THE SPIRIT WHO CALLS OUT "ABBA FATHER"
Ephesians 1:4-6; 2:18
James 1:16-18
1 John 3:1 SEE WHAT GREAT ♡ THE FATHER HAS LAVISHED ON US, THAT WE SHOULD BE CALLED CHILDREN OF GOD. THAT'S WHAT WE ARE. THE REASON THE WORLD DOESN'T KNOW US - IT DIDN'T KNOW HIM
Jude 1:1

ROM. 8: 15-17 SPIRIT (NOT SLAVES)=FEAR FATHER ADOPTION TO SONSHIP. CRY "Abba" Father. The Spirit himself testifies @ our spirit that we are children of God. Heirs - HEIRS of God & CO-HEIRS of Jesus Christ. - We share in his sufferings in order that we might share in His Glory.

As we discovered yesterday, God is addressed as "Father" by Jesus. Even though it's just a word to denote a particular person, it's a word laden with emotion as it can trigger different feelings in us because of our own experience with our father.

Maybe you have the best dad in the world. He loves you unconditionally, goes to all your basketball games, tells you he thinks you're awesome and is proud of you. You think your dad is amazing. *Or* you could feel deep pain as a result of your father and his actions (or lack of them). Maybe he bailed on you when you were a baby and your mom had to pick up all the pieces and has struggled to support you ever since. Maybe he's done things to you no one else knows about. The pain you feel has caused you to not only dislike your dad but to hate him. If that is you, I'm really sorry for all you've gone through, and so is God.

God is not like the kind of father you have experienced, whether he's a good father or not. Yes, your father can display characteristics of God's love and kindness, but he's not perfect and he makes mistakes. God is *the* perfect Father. Read James 1:16–18 a few times and in a few different translations. He doesn't change, He isn't fickle; He is consistently *good.* That is always, all the time, never-endingly *good.* What's more, we've been adopted into His family through simply believing, and we have access to Him *all* the time. James actually says He's given birth to us through the word of truth so we can be His prized possession (NLT). You are His beloved, His precious child, His favorite. Yes, you are His favorite. Now is that the kind of Father you can have an intimate relationship with? I *know* you can.

If you have had a challenging relationship with your earthly father, why don't you go to your heavenly Father and ask Him what you should do about it? I'm sure He'd love to tell you.

Do you have a special name you call your father? Dad, Daddy, Pop, Pa, Pappa? Have you ever thought of calling God one of those names? We can still come before Him in awe but at ease, sit on his lap, and say "Hey, Dad."

Spend some time with your Father God. Close your eyes and imagine going to Him and climbing onto His lap. What is He doing? What is He saying? You can use the journaling section at the back of the book to record what you hear.

STORY FROM LIFE

How Great the Father's Love

Chris grew up in a church-going family, but sometimes at home, life wasn't always great. His mom and dad fought a lot, and his dad worked long hours, sometimes away from home, so he felt like his dad didn't have much time for him or his little sister.

Chris loved God but struggled to love his dad because his dad never spent quality time with him, didn't go to his football games or ever say "I love you, son." Chris got to the point when he didn't even like his dad, especially because of the way he treated his mom.

Bitterness started to grow in his heart until it turned to hate. He was glad to finally leave home after finishing school. He still loved God, but he struggled to feel like God loved him, or that other people loved him, for that matter. He even started thinking other people hated him.

One day, a still small voice said in his mind, "You need to forgive your dad." He knew it was God. That day, he was able to forgive because he wanted to obey God. But he still struggled to believe the love of God for himself, until one day, he came across the verse in 1 John 3:1, "How great the love the Father has lavished on us, that we should become children of God. And that is what we are."

He kept that verse close to his heart, and every time he felt like he was forgotten or unloved, he returned to that verse until it finally started to sink in. Chris now lives in the freedom of a beloved son and he no longer hates his dad.

Can you relate to this story? Why don't you write your own story about your journey with your father? As you write, see if there is anything that comes up that you may need to address. For example:

- Do you need to forgive?
- Do you need to say sorry?
- Do you need to say thank you?

I praise & thank the Lord for my WONDERFUL, KIND, LOVING father ..... blessed beyond!

Thank you Lord, for giving me such an incredibly affectionate loving earthly father — my ♡ is full of thanksgiving

2 CHRON. 20:7 –

DAY

5

**Knowing
Jesus
as Friend**

Is. 41:8

READ

2 Chronicles 20:7
Isaiah 41:8
Matthew 11:19
John 15:9–17; 17:26
James 2:23 –

MATT. 11:19

JOHN 15:9–17
17:26

Do you have a friend you can talk with about absolutely anything? The kind who comes for sleepovers and you end up staying awake until 2 a.m. just talking and having fun together? What is it you like about this person? What makes it so easy to share your innermost thoughts and feelings with them? There are at least two characteristics I can think of that make us share in this way—trust and unconditional love with no judgment attached. You can trust them with your secrets—they won't go around spreading rumors about you. You can trust them to listen, to come through for you, to give good advice, and to love you no matter what.

It truly is an amazing blessing to have a good friend or two to share life's ups and downs with, but no matter how good a friend a person is, they still have the potential to let you down. But there is *One* who is a perfect friend who will never let you down. Just as God is the perfect Father, He is also the perfect friend. We can see this aspect of God displayed through the life of Jesus who, while being the Son of God, is also God (John 10:30, 37–38). I know it's a bit hard to get our heads around this concept, but trust me (and the Bible)—Jesus is God, and He said He no longer calls us His servants but His friends. He was also noted as being a friend of sinners. That sounds like non-judgment to me.

Jesus said there is no greater love than to lay down one's life for one's friends (John 15:13), and we know Jesus actually lived this out by dying for each and every one of us on the cross (Romans 5:8; 1 John 3:16). You can absolutely count on His love for you because He's already shown you how much He loves you through this act. So guess what. You can talk to Him openly, just as you talk to your best friend.

REFLECT

Have you ever spoken to Jesus as your best friend, or do you fear you can't trust Him? *Regularly.*

Trust in the Lord @ all your ♡ and lean NOT on your own understanding. In ALL your ways acknowledge Him & He will direct your path.

ACT

Search 'verses that speak about trusting in God' or His faithfulness on a search engine. Or if your Bible has a concordance, look up the verses that speak about trust and how dependable God is. Write down the ones that really stick out to you in the journal at the back of the book or in your own journal.

John 14:26 Holy Spirit — SENT IN JESUS NAME
— ADVOCATE
— TEACHER OF ALL THINGS.
— REMIND US OF JESUS' WORDS.

Filled a grief - as Jesus goes back to His Father.
16:5-15 Jesus sends the ADVOCATE. Convicts WRONG, +RIGHT, JUDGMT.
SPIRIT - GUIDES INTO ALL TRUTH, Spirit receives from Jesus makes KNOWN to us.

DAY
6

Knowing the Holy Spirit

READ

John 14:26; 16:5–15
Acts 10:19–21; 13:2
Philippians 2:1–2 — ENCOURAGMT. BEING UNITED ⓔ
CHRIST. COMFORT FROM HIS ♡.
SPIRIT ⟹ TENDERNESS
COMPASSION
Be like-minded (SAME ♡)
ONE IN SPIRIT / MIND

ACTS 10: 19-21
SPIRIT: SIMON 3 men looking for you. Get up, go downstairs
"I have sent them." looking for. Why have you come?
I am the one you are looking for. Why have you come?
Come from Cornelius: +Rom, God-fearing man, respected by
all Jews. Holy angel told him to ask you to come to his house.

ACTS 13:2 Worshipping / Fasting
Holy Spirit said ⟨19⟩ — Set apart Barnabas / Saul for work
to which I HAVE CALLED THEM.

Our journey so far has shown we can know God as Father and Jesus as friend, two out of the three persons of the Trinity (Father, Son, and Holy Spirit). That may make sense to you, as it can be easy to picture them as persons, but you may ask how you can have an intimate relationship with a spirit. Well, just as the Father and Son are real beings, the Holy Spirit is also a real being, just not one with a physical form. That is why we can say He is a person, even though He doesn't have a body like Jesus. Jesus called the Holy Spirit a "he" when telling His disciples about Him—that word is a singular, personal pronoun (if you've ever learned grammar in school, you'll know what that means—otherwise, Google it).

The Spirit isn't a vague, ghostly apparition with no personality, nor is He an energy force. He is a very real, powerful, holy (absolutely pure), comforting, helpful being who speaks. He isn't just a part of God, He is God. All this can be mind-blowing, and I don't understand the Trinity fully (I'm no theologian), but the Bible does make it clear the Holy Spirit is knowable. In fact, Philippians 2:1 says there is fellowship in the Spirit. There is so much to that word "fellowship" that is hard to convey in English, but think of it as sharing everything of yourself, an intimacy that is hard to describe in earthly words.

The Holy Spirit loves us, wants us to know Him too, and wants to guide us into all truth (and so much more, but let's leave that for another day).

Have you ever tried to purposefully talk to the Holy Spirit, not just God the Father or Jesus? How does it make you feel to address Him who is known as the third person of the Trinity?

Take a walk and as you go, ask the Holy Spirit to lead you. Talk to Him along the way. Ask questions such as, 'which way should I turn?', 'where do you want me to stop?', 'what do you want me to look at?'. Record your experience afterwards.

62:1-12 GOD - my soul rests in Him
- MY SALVATION/ROCK, FORTRESS - NEVER BE SHAKEN
- ENEMIES, TRY TO SHAKE ME.
- REST - HOPE. MIGHTY ROCK/SALVATION/REFUGE
- TRUST ALWAYS, POUR OUT ♡.
- DON'T SET YOUR ♡ ON RICHES
- POWERFUL, UNFAILING LOVE → REWARDS everyone - what they have done

PS. 81: 7-16
distress - called = RESCUE
X WORSHIP OTHER GODS.
I AM YOUR GOD -
PROVIDE (feed) YOU.
wouldn't LISTEN -
gave them up own desires
Don't listen/submit foes
turn ag. them = punishment
& God will satisfy

DAY
7

A Two-Way
Conversation

HEB. 1:1,2 - Before God spoke in times past - Prophets
Now speaks to us → His Son

READ

Psalm 62:1-12; 81:7-16
Jeremiah 7:23-26
John 10:1-18
Hebrews 1:1-2
1 Peter 3:12   EYES OF THE LORD ARE THOSE,
EARS ATTENTIVE - PRAYERS
FACE OF THE LORD - AG. THOSE WHO DO EVIL.

Jer. 7:23-26 OBEY ME = I WILL BE YOUR GOD - MY PEOPLE!
WALK IN OBED = ALL WILL BE WELL!
WOULDN'T LISTEN → BACKWARDS - will g∞d,
STIFF NECKED - more evil than ancestors

JOHN 10:1-18 Jesus - Gate of the Sheep ENTER = SALVATION
GOOD SHEPHERD - know my sheep - sheep know me
Jesus lays down his life for His sheep.

22

How are you traveling so far? I hope by this stage you are getting more excited about where this adventure is taking us. God is such a good Father, faithful friend, and great listener.

As we have already discovered, God is close and accessible and loves to hear everything about how we are feeling in life, even though He already knows it all. We can unashamedly pour out our hearts to Him and He is right there ready to respond. But, like in any relationship, if we were the only one doing the talking all the time, we wouldn't get to know what the other person was thinking or if they had any good advice for us. It would be a pretty boring relationship, don't you think?

Just as God is a good listener, we, too, need to learn to be good listeners. We have plenty of examples in the Bible of people who weren't good at listening to God, including the children of Israel. Being a good listener implies being a good follower, because we know from history that when the children of Israel didn't listen—therefore didn't follow—things didn't go well for them. Fortunately for us, we don't need Old Testament prophets anymore to speak God's words to us. We have the written Word of God and the living Word of God, Jesus (John 1), plus the promised Holy Spirit who leads and guides. God is always speaking, and we need to learn to tune in to His frequency to know what He is saying. So stay tuned to find out how we can do this. Yes, you can roll your eyes at this one. ☺

Has there been a time in your life when you were in trouble and you poured out your heart to God? What feeling did you have after you poured your heart out to Him? Did you sense anything God might have been saying back to you?

Has there been a time when you were in trouble, poured out your heart to God, and heard Him give advice about a situation, but you didn't listen to that advice? How did things turn out for you?

Is there something someone in authority in your life has asked you to do and you haven't followed through? Think about a time when you were disobedient to an earthly authority and ask God if you need to make it right and if so, how to do so.

Off-Roading Madness

I was in my mid-twenties. A weekend away camping with friends was just what the doctor ordered. I was studying and working in Melbourne at the time, so it was nice to get away into the bush at the back of my aunt and uncle's property in the foothills of North East Victoria.

We were a mixed bunch—some male Bible school friends, my female cousin, and another friend from Melbourne. The boys just wanted to spend the whole time hunting while the girls stayed closer to camp. On the last morning of camp, a Sunday, the boys hadn't had much success so they decided to head off early for another location to try their luck there. Us girls were left to pack up the rest of the camp into the borrowed four-wheel drive. But before we headed off, we wanted some adventure of our own.

The boys had told us of a track they had driven up the day before, and we thought *Why not try it? After all, what boys can do, girls can do better.* When we got to the aforementioned track, there was a sign saying Track Closed. There had been bushfires in the region not long before, and as a result, the tracks had become loose due to the destruction of surrounding vegetation.

But we were like, "Well, the boys did it so why can't we?" As we progressed along the track, it started getting steeper and steeper (picture Australian bush, in the mountains, with a rocky, gravelly, narrow, four-wheel drive track). On a steep ascent, I suddenly heard a pop and thought *Oh no!* Yep, a tire had punctured. Here we were, three girls, stuck on a steep four-wheel drive track in the middle of nowhere with a blown tire and no cell phone reception. And did I mention, the four-wheel drive was already packed to the brim with all our stuff? Guess where the spare tire was located. Yep, underneath it all.

Fortunately for us, my cousin is a practical farm girl, and she was under the vehicle in a jiffy, trying to jack it up. But the problem was we were on such a steep section that we couldn't jack it high enough. The large rocks by the edge of the road came in handy at that point as we were able to use them to raise the jack.

We, or should I say she, couldn't get the nuts off the tire so we were in a real pickle. I was by the vehicle praying, saying sorry to God for disobeying the sign, and feeling utterly helpless because I'm a weakling. Meanwhile, the plan of action was that my cousin would go by foot to my uncle and aunt's farmhouse to get the tools necessary. As it was a Sunday morning, they were off at church an hour down the road. The toolshed was locked, so my cousin had to break in.

Praise the Lord, my amazing cousin returned with the tools necessary and managed to change the tire. We were saved. And boy did I learn a lesson that day about listening and following (obeying). You see, I'd just been reading a book about the blessings of obedience based on Deuteronomy 28. I knew that in the context of the children of Israel, obedience brought blessings and disobedience brought curses. While I believe Jesus took every sin and curse upon Himself (Galatians 3:13) and we now live in a period of grace, being disobedient to the road sign—God's Word—can still have negative and damaging consequences. We need to then ask God for His help to get out of them. It's better to not get into that situation in the first place. I encourage you, no matter the temptation for adventure, to heed the signs God places in front of you. It's for your own good in the end.

DAY
8

**Tuning
in to
God's voice**

READ →

1 Samuel 3:1–10
Psalm 130

SAMUEL ASKED ELI "YOU CALLED ME"
ELI- "I DID NOT" 3x
SAMUEL SAY:
"Speak Lord for your
servant is listening.

Lord: SAMUEL, SAMUEL - SAMUEL -
Speak, for
your servant
is listening

Ps. 130: I cried to the Lord
Let your ears hear my cry for MERCY.
With You there is FORGIVENESS.
Wait in HOPE for the Lord (like watchman waiting for morning

Israel - Put your hope in You - UNFAILING ♡
FULL REDEMPTION

The Lord Himself will REDEEM Israel from ALL their sins.

"Okay, so God is always speaking, but how come *I* can't hear Him?" I'm glad you asked. The simple answer is you *can* hear Him, if you're tuned in. Listening to God is firstly a matter of *wanting* to hear Him. Just as there is always something playing on the radio, you can't hear what's playing until you choose to turn the radio on and tune in to the right frequency for the radio station you want to listen to. And just like there are many stations you can tune into, there are many voices vying for your attention, and they aren't always God's voice.

It took me a long time to tune in to the right frequency to hear God. I always knew the Word of God, the Bible, was the primary way God speaks to us, and I read it voraciously. I loved, and still do love, the Word of God, but it took until my twenties to realize He wants to speak to us in other ways too, as long as there is a precedent for it in the Word of God. In my mid-twenties, I was in Bible school in Canada seeking God for what He wanted me to do in the future. I was a teacher and thought maybe He wanted me to be a missionary teacher in a third world nation. I did a mission trip to Mexico as part of my Bible school training, and I was so frustrated at not being able to speak the language. Not being a huge language person, I was like, "God, I don't know if I could do it." The first week back at Bible school after the trip, the teaching was from Ezekiel, and during the reading of it, a verse popped straight out from the page, "For you are not sent to a people of foreign speech and a hard language, but to the house of Israel—not to many peoples of foreign speech and a hard language, whose words you cannot understand" (Ezekiel 3:5–6). Hahaha. I had my answer and boy, did I feel relief. God used a combination of circumstances and His Word to speak.

Listening to God is a position of the heart. Yes, there are times when God will miraculously get our attention, even when we aren't asking for it, as in the case of Saul on the road to Damascus (Acts 9:3–6). However, most of the time it is up to us to make a choice to posture our heart to want to hear from God. We consciously choose to still ourselves from the noise around us and say, "Lord, what do you want to say to me?"

Did you notice Samuel thought Eli was talking to him? Have there been times in your life when you heard a voice and thought it was someone else speaking to you, only to realize God was trying to get your attention? What was your response?

Find a quiet spot, whether it's in a park, in a quiet room, or even in a car. Take a journal, a Bible and a pen with you. Turn off your phone and all other distractions. Ask, 'Lord, what do you want to say to me? Your servant is listening.' Be still...it may take a moment, it may take minutes, but keep on seeking until you sense the Lord speaking. Record what He says. If you aren't aware of Him saying anything in particular, open your Bible and see if there are any verses that stand out to you and write them down.

1 KINGS 19:11-13 GO MOUNTAIN - the Lord will pass by.
GREAT WIND... Lord not there.
EARTHQUAKE.... Lord not there
FIRE.... Lord not there
↳ GENTLE WHISPER - "What are you doing
                                        there,
                                        ELIJAH!

Acts 10:33
An angel spoke to
Cornelius - sent for
Peter vision
sheet / all animals
get up & eat.
Don't call anything
unclean, God has
called CLEAN. (3X)
God does NOT
show favouritism - accepts all who do RIGHT.

DAY
9

Is That
You, God?

2 Cor 4:4
GOD HAS
BLINDED THE
EYES OF
UNBELIEVER!

READ

1 Kings 19:11-13
Mark 4:9 WHOEVER HAS EARS TO HEAR -
            LET HIM HEAR.
Luke 4:1-13
John 8:44
Acts 10:1-33
Romans 12:2 DO NOT CONFORM TO THIS WORLD
                    TRANSFORMED BY THE
2 Corinthians 4:4 RENEWING OF YOUR MIND
                          YOU CAN TEST / APPROVE WHAT IS
                                              GODS WILL.

LUKE 4:1-13
Lord full of H.Sp. - lead by Spirit.
STONES - BREAD "Man shall not live by bread alone."
WORSHIP ME "Worship the Lord God & serve Him only"
THROW YOURSELF DOWN "Do not put the Lord God to the test"
Devil finished — LEFT.

John 8:44 Jesus said, You belong to your Father devil,
He is a MURDERER, ㉜ LIAR!

As suggested yesterday, there can be many voices
vying for our attention, so how do we know which
one is God's and which ones are not? What are these
other voices? The voices I'm speaking about often
sound like our very own thoughts and can be from
the devil, the world around us, or ourselves. *VOICES*

We see in Luke 4 that the devil can speak. He spoke
to Jesus to tempt Him while He was fasting for forty
days in the wilderness, and the way he tempted Him
was by using doubt, as shown by the statements "If
you…" He used the same trick in the garden of Eden
with Adam and Eve when he said, "Did God actually
say…?" (Genesis 3:1). He is also called the father of
lies, and everything he speaks to us is a lie. You'll
know it's the devil when what you hear makes you
question what God has really said, so you
investigate, only to find it doesn't line up with the *DEVIL*
truth of Scripture.

The world holds the prevailing thought of the age we
live in, the common culture that surrounds us that
says certain things are or aren't okay. Most of the
time, the culture of the world around us doesn't line
up with the Word of God, and that is why Paul said
we need to be transformed by the renewal of our
mind so we may discern the will of God.

Our own desires, often talked of as "the flesh" in the
Bible, also speak to us. When we are born again, we
have purified desires, but sometimes sin still comes
crouching at our door (see Genesis 4:7), which makes
us think certain thoughts that aren't in line with
God's.

So what does God sound like? Well, we can answer that from what He does *not* sound like. He doesn't sound angry or condemning, nor does He give us anxious thoughts. It is often through the still, small voice that we hear God. His voice sometimes sounds like a soft whisper, but as the Bible says, He can speak through dreams, visions, angels, creation, circumstances, or other people. What you think He's saying must always line up with what Scripture tells us. Just as we learn to recognize the voice of someone we love the more we spend time with them, so we will learn to recognize God's voice as we get to know Him better.

Take time to consider the different ways God can and does speak. Do you feel more comfortable with some ways than others? *All Ways!*

Get together with a Christian friend, family member, youth leader or a mentor. Tell them you are learning to hear the voice of God and want to practice with them. Pray together and ask God to give you a specific word of encouragement for the other person. It may come to mind in the form of a scripture verse, an image, a word or sentence or a deep impression. Share with that person to get their feedback and to see if it resonates with them. If it doesn't, don't worry. Keep practicing!

Learning How God Speaks

When I was about eighteen years old, I went to a youth camp for at-risk young people, my very first involvement with Youth for Christ as a leader. I had grown up in a very sheltered environment in a country town. During a time with other leaders at camp, the question about how God speaks to us came up. The only answer I had was "through the Bible." Even though I'd been a Christian from a very young age, I didn't know any other way.

It was not until my mid-twenties, when I began having very vivid dreams, that I discovered maybe there were other ways of God speaking. After having three very vivid dreams in a row, I got to the point of being on my knees, crying out to God, "I know you spoke to people in the Bible through dreams, so if you're trying to speak to me, you'd better show me what these dreams are about." That set me on a journey to find out all I could about knowing how God speaks. I was also blessed to have a couple of very good mentors in my life who I was able to share all my thoughts and concerns with.

One book that really helped me was *Surprised by the Voice of God* by Jack Deere.[2] If you would love to discover more on this topic, I encourage you to find a

---

[2] Deere, Jack, *Surprised by the Voice of God: How God Speaks Today Through Prophecies, Dreams, and Visions.* (Kingsway, 1996).

copy and have a read. It may be a turning point in your relationship with God. I know it was for me. God is so good, and it's important for us to know this when discovering God's voice. He doesn't want to frighten us or cause us grief. He speaks to us because He loves us and wants the best for us and His church. So why not open yourself up to the various ways He wants to speak to you? I guarantee, it will be a lifelong adventure if you are only willing to say "Speak, for your servant is listening" (1 Samuel 3:10).

Ps. 25: 11-15 FORGIVE MY GREAT INIQUITY, INSTRUCT ME IN THE WAY
I SHOULD GO, AS I FEAR YOU. SPEND DAYS IN
PROSPERITY — HEIR INHERIT LAND.
LORD CONFIDES IN THOSE WHO FEAR HIM
LORD MAKES HIS COV. KNOWN TO THEM.

My eyes are forever on the Lord - He will release my feet from the snare.

DAY 10

Are You a Trustworthy Friend?

READ — Psalm 25:11–15
John 15:14–17; 17:6; 21:15–22

John 15: 14-17 — You are my friends if you do my commands. I call you friends (not servants) for I have made everything that my Father told me to you. I chose you to bear FRUIT - FRUIT that will LAST, whatever you ask in my name - I will give you. This is my command "Love one another"

John 17:6 — Jesus revealed God to us. They are yours - you gave them to me. They have obeyed your word.

John 21: 15-22 — JESUS REINSTATES PETER:
① SIMON PETER - do you ♡ me.
YES - You know I ♡ you - FEED MY SHEEP.
② DO YOU - YES - take care of my sheep.
③ Do you ♡ me - you know I ♡ you - KNOW ALL THINGS -

Feed My sheep.

We have discovered God is a trustworthy friend to us, but are we a trustworthy friend to God? Did you notice in Psalm 25:14 that King David says the friendship of the Lord is for those who fear Him— those who revere Him and really desire to worship Him and Him alone. Another way friendship can be translated in this passage is "secret counsel." The word Jesus used to call his disciples "friends" in John 15 is also used to describe the inner circle around a king or emperor; the friends of the king would be close to him and know his secrets.[3] God wants to share His secrets with His friends.

FEAR
REVERE
WORSHIP

Lord, I'm listening

It is amazing God would want to trust us as His friend. Most of what He wants to say to us is clearly revealed through the Word of God—it is plain for everyone to know—and you may hear Him say things to you that are already found in Scripture. But sometimes He wants to show you things that are not direct revelation from Scripture, things that pertain to situations or circumstances going on in the world that are not known to everyone.

At one time in my life, over a period of a few weeks, I had dreams concerning a person I'll call Rick. I would ask God to show me what these dreams meant and what to do with the information. Most of the time, I was just to pray for Rick. Then one day, I felt led to encourage him by writing him a letter and sharing what I felt God wanted to speak to him. It was pretty scary for me at the time, but when he read it, he confirmed everything in it was correct and said,

---

[3] Wiersbe, Warren W. *Bible Exposition Commentary, Vol. 1: New Testament,* (Chariot Victor Pub; 2nd edition, 2003), 357.

"If I had gotten this letter a couple of weeks ago, I would have torn it up." God's timing is perfect. In this instance, God wanted to share with me another person's secret so I could pray for him and bring encouragement. God knew He could trust me not to gossip about this person or share his secrets with others. Wow, what a privilege.

We won't always get it right. God is merciful and forgiving and gives us numerous chances to show we are trustworthy, just as Jesus did with Peter, who denied Him three times. As we grow in intimacy with God, He is sure to tell us some things He wants to keep between us as friends. Guard the trust He has in you, just as a friend of a king enjoys intimacy with him but also needs to be obedient to him.

Are you a trustworthy friend to your earthly friends? Can you keep their secrets or is this a challenge for you? I encourage you to develop your trustworthiness with your earthly friends and see how that impacts your relationship with God as a friend.

ACT

Has there been a time when you have broken trust
with a friend by sharing something they have shared
with you with someone else when you shouldn't
have? Write a letter to God and/or this friend to ask
for forgiveness.

Spend some time thanking God that He calls us
friends and ask Him to help you be a better friend to
Him and to others.

Father, thank You for being my
forever BEST friend. I love
You, adore You and feel so
BLESSED & PRIVILEGED to have
You as my faithful, kind &
loving friend.
May I be a loyal, faithful friend
to You & others around. May the
words of my mouth & meditation
of my ♡ please You Lord.
You are my joy
& my Salvation!

Tools for Intimacy: Prayer Practice

Journaling

Take a pen and paper out and ask God to speak to you about anything He wants to say. Just wait in silence for a moment. Often the first thought that comes to mind is *I love you.* Start with that and see what flows. You may think you're hearing your own thoughts, but God uses our faculties to speak to us.

Write your thoughts, feelings, and prayers to God. Journaling is a great way to pour out your heart to Him (Psalm 62:8). When you have expressed yourself, pause and see if there's anything He wants to respond to you with.

Prayer walking

Do you walk regularly? Imagine Jesus is walking with you. What do you want to share with Him? What does He share back?

Hanging out

You like to go to certain places and just hang out with your friends, so why not set aside a morning or afternoon to go to a special place and hang out with Jesus? Maybe you can take your journal and Bible and hang out at a café, by a river, or at the beach. If you enjoy the arts, take a sketchbook or paints. You don't have to just sit there and meditate. Enjoy doing things with Him.

Lectio Divina

Lectio Divina is Latin for "divine reading."[4] It is a method of reflective reading and prayer that leads us into the deeper meaning of Scripture and the transformation of our lives. It's best to choose a short, familiar passage of Scripture, no more than ten verses long. You could try starting with Isaiah 55:1–5, Psalm 23, Mark 10:46–52, or Psalm 62:1–8. There are four stages:

- **Read** it out loud, slowly. Take your time. Repeat it two or three times. Listen with the "ear" of your heart. What word or phrase stands out to you?

- **Reflect** on the word or phrase, repeating it over and over, allowing it to settle deeply in your heart. Don't try to analyze it. Simply savor it. Let an attitude of quiet receptiveness permeate the prayer time. Be attentive to what you sense the Lord speaking to your heart.

- **Respond** to the Lord as you continue to repeat and savor the word or phrase. A prayer of praise or petition may arise. Offer that prayer to the

---

[4] Leonhardt, Douglas J. "Praying with Scripture," *Ignatian Spirituality.* www.ignatianspirituality.com. (Accessed November 11, 2020.) Further citations of this work are given in the text.

Lord and then return to repeating the word or phrase in your heart.

- **Rest** in God. Sit still in the presence of God. Is there a thought or feeling you have at the end of this experience? Journal what God impressed upon you.

Gospel contemplation

A prayerful and imaginative way of reading and reflecting on Scripture.

- Choose a passage from the Gospels (Matthew, Mark, Luke, and John) where Jesus is interacting with others.

- Ask God to be present and speak to you through His Word.

- Read through the selected passage at least twice, until the story becomes familiar.

- Close your eyes and imagine the scene. Engage it with all your senses. What do you see? Smell? Hear? Touch? Taste?

- Focus on Jesus. What is He doing? What is He saying? How is He interacting with others?

- Focus on the crowd. How are they reacting to Jesus? What are they saying? What emotions are they feeling?

- Focus on yourself. Where are you in the scene? How is Jesus interacting with you? How are you responding?

- Close with prayer. Spend some time talking to God about what you experienced through the story.

Worship and prayer

Turn your affection toward God by playing some worship music. Just enjoy being in His presence, or begin singing with the worship music. As you still yourself before Him in worship, ask if there's anything He'd like to share with you.

Part 2

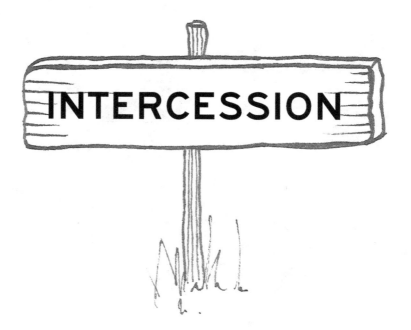

INTERCESSION

John 17: 9-17 I pray for them that are mine. I am going to you.
Father → PROTECT them by your power - so they can be
one as we are one. I protected them & kept them safe
All but one doomed (Scripture) would be fulfilled.
Saying these things - so they might have the FULL JOY within them.
Protect them
they are not of this
from the evil one.
world as I am not.
SANCTIFY THEM
YOUR WORD IS TRUTH.
BY YOUR TRUTH.

DAY
11

Intercession: a Get-To

John 17 (20-21) → I pray for them & those who believe the
mess → them. that all may be ONE
Just as you are in ME & I am in them.
May they also be in us, so that the world will
believe that you sent ME.

READ
John 17:9-17, 20-21
1 Timothy 2:1-5
Hebrews 7:25
HE IS ABLE TO SAVE COMPLETELY
THOSE WHO COME TO GOD THROUGH HIM BECAUSE
HE ALWAYS LIVES TO INTERCEDE FOR THEM.

1 Tim 2:1-5 Petitions / prayers / intercession & thanksgiving
be made for ALL people, so they may live
a quiet life in all godliness & holiness
This is good & pleases God our Savior ... who wants
ALL people to be saved & come to the knowledge of the truth
ONE GOD / ONE MEDIATOR between God & man → Christ Jesus.
who gave himself as a ransom for ALL people.
I was appointed as a TRUE & FAITHFUL teacher of the
Gentiles.

Part 2 of our adventure is about to begin. How are you traveling so far? Are you having fun with Jesus? I hope so. Over the next ten days, we'll be exploring what intercession is and how to do it effectively.

If you have ever asked God to help someone else, then you have participated in the act of intercession. While the word "intercession" *does* exist in the Bible, it only comes up a couple of times; however, we use it in Christianese because of its English meaning, which is "the action of intervening on behalf of another; the action of saying a prayer on behalf of another."[5]

The original Greek for the word "intercession" is just another way to say prayer or supplication—seeking, asking, entreating God. We see in John 17 that Jesus, while He was chatting away to His Father about His life on earth and His disciples, switched to intercession to pray *for* His disciples and those who would believe in the future—which includes us. That is pretty much how intercession works—it flows out of our relationship with God.

On day 1, I asked you to reflect on your view of prayer. When I was young, I thought prayer was about having a big long list of things or people to pray through each day. Once I'd gotten through the list, my job was done and then I was able to get on with the rest of my day. Yes, I treated it more like a

---

[5] "Definition of intercession". Oxford University Press. Lexico.com. (Accessed: 25 January 2021). https://www.lexico.com/definition/intercession

task I "had" to complete rather than something I "got" to do out of a love relationship with God. It was so freeing to know that praying for others is something that comes naturally when we see our Christian life as a relationship with God and others rather than a set of rules to live by. We don't *have to* have a list of things to pray through in order to fulfill a Christian duty. The people, places, or circumstances we *get* to pray for will be made evident to us as we live in intimacy with our Father. That makes intercession an adventure with God.

Is the way you view prayer changing as you learn more each day?

Write down what you have learned on your journey so far and how that may be different to what you thought when you started out.

JOHN 15:1-17 - THE VINE - Jesus SUSTENANCE, LIFE TO BRANCHES
GARDNER God - prunes! PRUNING!
Remain in me = BEAR FRUIT
APART FROM ME YOU ARE NOTHING. NOT IN ME = THROWN IN FIRE/BURNED.
BEAR FRUIT = PROVING MY DISCIPLES.
FATHER HAS ♡ ME - / ♡ YOU. KEEP COMMANDS → REMAIN IN MY ♡.
COMMAND: ♡ ONE ANOTHER
CALL YOU FRIENDS.
CHOSE/APPOINTED YOU TO
BEAR FRUIT. whatever you
ask My Father will give.

♡) EACH OTHER !

16: 23-24
Father will give you
anything you ask in
My name.
Ask - RECEIVE, joy will
be complete.

DAY
12
ABIDE IN ME !
What's in the
Power of
a Name?

17: 22,23
I'm coming to
YOU, FATHER.
PROTECT THEM
BY THE POWER
OF YOUR NAME -
SO THEY CAN BE
ONE AS WE ARE
ONE.
NONE LOST !

READ → John 15:1-17; 16:23-24; 17:11-12
Acts 3:6-16; 4:30

ACTS 3: 6-16 - IN THE NAME OF JESUS - Walk. Instantly feet & ankles
were made WHOLE. WALKING/LEAPING/PRAISING God.
PEOPLE FILLED @ WONDER/ AMAZEMENT.
PETER ASKED - Why amazed - power of Jesus Christ. You killed &
disowned Jesus. By Jesus' name & faith this man is healed.

4:30 After praying - the meeting place was shaking. And
they were FILLED @ the Holy Spirit & spoke the
word of God BOLDLY. 50

Have you ever wondered why people say "in Jesus's name" at the end of a prayer? Is it a magic formula by which our prayers are answered? (The answer, of course, is no.)

In the Bible, a name means so much more than just what someone is called. For example, the name Isaac means "laughter" because when God told Abraham and Sarah they would have a child in their old age, they laughed (Genesis 17:17; 18:11–15). The name Jesus comes from the Hebrew *Joshua* which means "Jehovah is salvation"—it reveals He is the Savior (Matthew 1:21). A name not only reveals the nature of someone but the authority, reputation, and power they carry.[6] For example, when the President or Prime Minister of a country gives an order to someone, they know it needs to be obeyed because their name indicates they have the authority to make something happen. So when we pray "in the name of Jesus," we are calling upon all His name means—His power and authority—for all authority has been given to Him (Matthew 28:18).

When we pray, Jesus makes things happen (Acts 3:12–16). John 15 talks about Jesus being the vine and the disciples being the branches. The vine is what brings sustenance and life to the branches—the branches can only produce fruit when they remain in the vine. This is why intimacy is the key to our prayers. We must stay connected with Jesus and walk in obedience to Him so we receive *His* authority. It is not our own authority; it is His

---

[6] Wiersbe, Warren W. *Bible Exposition Commentary, Vol. 1: New Testament,* (Chariot Victor Pub; 2nd edition, 2003), 411.

authority in us. We can ask in His name and it will be done. Now that's a lot of power.

Think about the way Jesus demonstrated His authority on the earth through healing, deliverance, miracles, and teaching. How does it make you feel to know that, as a believer, you have the authority of Jesus to ask things in His name? *SUPPORTED LOVED - ENCOURAGED, BLESSED ABUNDANTLY!*

Ask the Lord to show you a situation or circumstance right now that seems impossible to you. Remembering the authority you possess in Jesus, pray for that situation or circumstance to shift. If it's a particular person you have in mind, ask the Lord if you should approach them to pray for them in person.

Lord, I pray for Dan this morning. Please provide a CARING, HEALING, SUPPORTIVE caregiver so that he might get the help he so desperately needs to start healing & moving forward. A med. worker w unbelievable compassion & kindness. Pour out your Mercy & Grace! If we have an opportunity - may we be able to visit & pray @ Dan!

PHIL 4:6 – DON'T BE ANXIOUS ABOUT anything
BUT IN every SITUATION
BY PRAYER & PETITION @ THANKSGIVING!
make your requests known (PRESENT YOUR
REQUESTS)

First of All...

PRAYER

PRAY: ALL OCCASIONS/ALL KINDS OF PRAYERS/REQUESTS
BE ALERT- KEEP PRAYING. PRAY FOR PAUL
BOLD – WDS GIVEN FEARLESSLY MADE KNOWN

READ

Ephesians 6:18–20 GOSPEL
Philippians 4:6
1 Timothy 2:1–4
Hebrews 5:7

1 Tim. 2:1-4 ALL PETITIONS, PRAYERS INTERCESSION &
THANKSGIVING BE MADE FOR ALL PEOPLE –
KINGS, THOSE IN AUTHORITY. peaceful/
quiet life
IN ALL GODLINESS & HOLINESS.
This please God, our Saviour, who
wants all people saved & come to a
knowledge of the TRUTH.

Heb. 5:7 In Jesus' life → He offered up prayers
& petitions @ FERVENT CRIES/TEARS
to the One 53 who could save Him from
death & He was heard because of His
reverent submission

Have you ever imagined putting yourself in the shoes of someone in the first-century church, hearing the words of people like the apostle Paul for the very first time? If you have, you would have heard the encouragement to pray often. Paul prayed for people constantly—there are too many scriptures to reference here—and he wanted those he taught to pray too. In fact, Paul valued prayer so much that when he was writing to his young charge Timothy, he told him this was the first priority (1 Timothy 2:1). He *urged* him. I can almost feel what Paul was feeling when he wrote: a sense of urgency, a "Come on, Timothy," a plea coming from his innermost being.

Paul often used the words "prayer" and "supplication" together. What's the difference?

- The word for prayer here comes from the word *"worship"* and expresses earnest prayer to God.

- Supplication is a wanting or a need, seeking and *asking* God for something specific.

Paul requested supplication for all people, kings, all who are in high positions, all the believers, and himself—as he proclaimed the gospel, among others.

When we think of all the people in the world, our brothers and sisters in Christ, it might get a little overwhelming to know what to pray for and how to pray. But often there are things that burn on our heart, things that get us "fired up" that we can bring before God.

If you get stuck, start with praying for "kings and all who are in high positions," or in other words, those who have authority in your city or nation. Another starting point could be to think about what makes you feel anxious. Paul said to not be anxious about anything, but to make requests to God with thanksgiving (Philippians 4:6). We can be specific in what we ask for, even though God knows every circumstance.

Listen to God.
Talk less / listen much.

Is there a "wanting" or a need deep inside you, something that is really stirring you at the moment? In whatever way you like—through journaling, art, poetry, or verbal prayer—make a request to God to express that desire.

If you don't already know, find out the names of the people in positions of authority in your nation and local government area, for example your President or Prime Minister, your State or Provincial governor/leader and your Mayor. Ask a friend or family member to join you in praying for these people on a regular basis. Or you may like to find a group in your area that specifically prays for governmental leaders.

Adding Legs to My Prayers

For over ten years, a passion for walking alongside First Nations Australians stirred me to pray for these precious, marginalized peoples. As I got to know God better, He started sharing His heart, through the Word and other people, for the poor and disenfranchised in the world. He made me aware that some of the most vulnerable people in the world were in my own backyard. I knew very little of our shared history, and the more I got to know, the more I asked myself why I didn't learn any of it in school.

I joined with others in praying for our First Nations Christian leaders, asking God to strengthen them, provide for them, and lead them. Pretty soon, my prayers led to action; it was not enough to pray. I began to advocate—with a campaign—to raise awareness of the gaps between First Nations people and other Australians in the areas of health, education, housing, mortality rates, and incarceration. It was a big learning curve. One day, I felt God prompt me with this thought: *If I'm going to advocate for these people, I want to be with them, to know them.* That led me on a journey to where I could begin relating with First Nations people. Pretty soon, I found myself volunteering in an Aboriginal school in the Northern Territory of Australia, and a year and a half later, I made the move from Australia's second largest city in the south, Melbourne, to Australia's smallest capital city in the far north, Darwin, and its remote outposts.

While you can find First Nations people in every corner of Australia, the people of the Northern Territory were where I found my extended family—adopted mums, brothers, sisters, daughters, sons. I was able to pray for them firsthand and see God move in ways I'd never seen before. My supplications and requests were given legs as God led me to be part of the answer to my own prayers. He has a habit of doing that. Yes, prayer in and of itself is powerful, but prayer with legs is even more so.

I need to pray more for Muskrat Dan. Diana / Todd - leaders, children, teachers, residences - ESTHER, PEGGY, MARY, CYRNA, JOB, GABRIEL,

Dan 10:1-14 VISION TO DAN. - GREAT WAR MOURNED 3 DAYS.
VISION MAN - others terrified/hid. Sleep.
Daniel highly esteemed - WANTED UNDERSTANDING - humble.
I will explain what will happen to your people.

DAY
14
Persistent
Prayer

PRAYER FOR ALL
BELIEVERS 8

John 17:20-21
My prayer is not
for them alone. I
pray also for them
who will believe
in me → their message,
THAT ALL MAY BE ONE
Father, just as you
are in me & I am
in you. — so the world
will believe you sent me.

Rom. 8:26-34.
Spirit helps us in
our weakness.
Spirit intercedes
with for us →
wordless groans
He who searches
hearts & knows the
mind of Spirit
Spirit intercedes
for God's people
in accordance
w/ God's will.
We know ALL
things work for good - called accord.
to His purposes. Predestined to
conform to image of His Son. If God
is for us - who can be
against us. God
justifies. Right hand of
God intercedes for
us.

READ →
Daniel 10:1-14
Luke 18:1-8; 22:39-46
John 17:20-21
Romans 8:26-34

Luke 18:1-8 PARABLE OF PERSISTANT Widow
UNGODLY JUDGE - widow - justice ag. enemy.
BECAUSE widow keeps bothering me → JUSTICE.
Will not God bring justice to those who cry out day & night.
He will see they get justice/quickly. FAITH!

Luke 22:39-46 MT. of Olives - "Pray you will not fall into
temptation
"Father, if you are willing, take this cup from me.
YET not my will but yours be done." An angel appeared &
strengthened Him. Being in anguish SWEAT DROPS of BLOOD
Went to disciples "WHY ARE YOU SLEEPING?" PRAY - so you will not fall
into temptation

58

But I have prayed and prayed and nothing has changed. Have you ever had that thought? I have. What happens when we commit ourselves to pray for a person or situation and it remains the same, or it gets worse? Discouragement can be a natural consequence of seeing prayer unanswered, but the Lord encourages us to "always pray and not lose heart" (Luke 18:1).

I once heard a preacher tell the story of a lady at his church who always kept a seat free beside her. Whenever someone wanted to go and sit in that seat, she shooed them off and said it was taken. She was considered the grumpy, unfriendly lady of the church. This went on for decades until finally, one Sunday, the people realized why that seat was left vacant. In came an elderly man who sat down beside her. You see, she had been praying for her husband every day for decades, and eventually he gave his life to the Lord and began attending church with her. Pretty soon, the whole row was filled with her family members.[7]

God is a faithful God, and He calls us to be faithful in prayer. Yes, we will sometimes feel discouraged and feel like giving up, but we may be just one prayer away from breakthrough. As we pray, the ultimate goal is to see God's will done. Jesus wished the cup of suffering—the journey to death on a cross—could be taken away from Him, but He was willing to surrender fully to the Father's plan. His death wasn't

---

[7] This may not be a 100 percent accurate retelling of the story, but it gives the picture.

the final word on the matter. Three days later He rose to victorious life, and this sacrificial act was the turning point of history—people can be saved once and for all from the power of sin and death.

So next time you feel like giving up, do yourself a favor and remember a couple of things: Jesus paid the highest price for you to know Him *and* He is alive at the right hand of God right now interceding for you. God's Word promises that as we pray, even when we don't know how, the Holy Spirit and Jesus are also interceding and God is working all things together for good (Romans 8:28). He has not given up and neither should you.

REFLECT

Think about one person or situation you've been praying for for a long time without seeing any change. Ask God to show you how He views this person's situation. What is He telling you?

My brother Stephen + Jana → SALVATION. Keep praying. Thank You Lord, for hearing my many prayers for my brother. It's a great reminder that You are interceding on their behalf * YOUR TIME → YOUR WAY!

ACT

Wait on the Lord (be still and with a listening heart)
and ask Him who is someone He wants you to
commit praying for over the long term (e.g. friend,
relative or member of your immediate family) or to
recommit to praying for. You may initially commit to
praying for them for six months so it doesn't seem
overwhelming. Share this commitment with a
reliable Christian you trust, such as your youth
pastor or leader, and ask them to check in with you
now and then how your praying is going and what
you have seen the Lord doing in this person or in
you over time.

My brother Stephen! Ina & SALVATION
My sister-in-law Ina & SALVATION

I Kings 17:1-7 ELIJAH ANNOUNCES A GREAT DROUGHT.
ELIJAH goes to ravine-drink Ravens will feed you.
Later brook dried up - NO RAIN in land.

IK. 18:41-45 Elijah said to Ahab, Go, EAT/DRINK sound of heavy
rain 44 Elijah said go look towards the sea
(to servant)
7th x - small cloud.
ELIJAH
& tell Ahab ran
ahead of Ahab to
JEZREEL.

DAY 15

Prayer of the Righteous

READ   1 Kings 17:1-7; 18:41-~~46~~
James 5:13-18
1 John 1:9; 3:7
2 Corinthians 5:21

James 5:13-18 · PRAYER of FAITH
TROUBLE- pray HAPPY-sing praises SICK- elders, anoint @ oil.
Prayer offered in faith will make sick person well. Lord will
raise them up. SIN- forgiven. Confess SIN- pray for each other
THE PRAYER OF A FROUS MAN AVAILETH MUCH. (powerful/effective)
ELIJAH- prayed 3½ yrs EARNESTLY - NO RAIN → He prayed
heaven gave RAIN - earth produced crops.

1 John 1:9 CONFESS OUR SINS - God is faithful/just - forgive
cleanse from all
unteness.
3:7 Don't let anyone lead you astray - the one who does
what is right = RIGHTEOUS - just as He is righteous.

The second part of James 5:16 may be one of the best-known verses in the New Testament: "The prayer of a righteous person is powerful and effective" (NIV). James then goes on to share a little story from the Old Testament about Elijah, who said it wouldn't rain except by his word (1 Kings 17:1), and it didn't rain until three and a half years later (1 Kings 18:45). Wow!

What is it to be a righteous person? In the simplest sense, it is a person who is right with God—one who is pure and holy, as God is (1 John 3:7). Righteousness is a study in itself, and YFC Australia even developed a whole school around this very important topic. It is vital as it speaks to our identity as sons and daughters of God. If we have been born again, we have been cleansed of all unrighteousness, and this means we are like God (1 John 4:17)—a big statement but it's true.[8] Perhaps one of the greatest strategies of Satan, the adversary, is to get us to *not* believe this truth. If we don't believe we are righteous as believers, then we won't live victorious, powerful lives.

When James says "Elijah was a human being, even as we are" (James 5:17), it just means Elijah was a human with certain feelings and passions. 2 Kings also makes it clear he was a man of God (2 Kings 1:10–12). Despite the human nature that gets in the way sometimes—the one that has feelings and emotions that don't always align with God's, it

---

[8] To see some teaching from the school about righteousness, go to Youth for Christ Australia's YouTube channel and watch "Mark Greenwood - Jesus is the truth about YOU (Jesus School Melbourne 2017)." https://www.youtube.com/watch?v=3PtCP6qpomc.

doesn't mean we aren't righteous; it just means we need to grow in our understanding of what we have become in God. I encourage you, believe who God says you are and you will find yourself praying powerful and effective prayers.

REFLECT

*I fail. I focus.
I'm not disappointed.
I often disappoint
myself God.
My God*

What do you think when you hear you are like God in this world—holy, righteous, pure? What things might you be believing that don't align with this truth?

ACT

Ask God to reveal to you any lies about what you are currently believing and ask Him to reveal the truth to you instead. Write the lie down and then write the truth of God next to it. You may have to look up Bible verses or talk to a mentor to help you.

Want More? *Remind me often Lord:*

*You are
HOLY, + RIGHTEOUS
PURE ....
& so am I
(EVEN WHEN I
DON'T FEEL IT)*

Read Mark Greenwood's book *Awake to Righteousness.*[9]

Thank you Lord!

---

[9] Greenwood, Mark. *Awake to Righteousness: A Life-Changing Look at the Substance of Salvation.* (Saints by Nature Publishing, 2017).

MATT. 17:14-20 Lord have mercy - SEIZURES disciples couldn't heal. Jesus rebuked the demon. Disciples asked: WHY couldn't we heal. "LITTLE FAITH" If you have faith of a mustard seed - say to mt. move - it will move. Nothing will be impossible for you!

MATT. 21:18-22
Fig tree - nothing except leaves.
MAY YOU NEVER BEAR FRUIT AGAIN. Immed. it withered.
FAITH - you too can do TO FIG TREE.
Say mt. throw yourself into the sea - DONE.
IF YOU BELIEVE: you will receive whatever you ask for in prayer.

DAY
16

You've Got to Have Faith

Rom. 4:18-22
fig. all hope, Abraham in hope BELIEVED & he became father of many nations. Body - good as dead 100 yrs. Sarah womb was dead.
- DIDN'T WAVER (God's promise) = STRENGTH FAITH
- GLORY TO GOD.
It was accredited to him as tRness: + us who believe (death/resurrection of Jesus)

READ

Matthew 17:14–20; 21:18–22
John 14:12–14
Romans 4:18–22
James 5:13–15

James 5:13-15
TROUBLE - pray!
HAPPY - praise
SICK - elders pray - anoint oil.
A prayer offered in faith will make sick well. The Lord will raise them up. If sinned - FORGIVEN.
∴ confess your sins one to another & pray for each other so that you may be healed.
THE PRAYER OF A RIGHTEOUS MAN AVAILETH MUCH. (powerful/effective)

I was tempted to make allusions to a 1980s hit song called "Faith" in this title, but after hearing the lyrics, I changed my mind. It's not the kind of faith you want … trust me. But what is this faith the Bible talks about that is required for our prayer to be effective?

The Greek word for faith is *pistis* and can have the meanings of "assurance, belief, faith, and fidelity." It is a conviction of the truth. But it is not a faith in *anything;* it is a faith in the *person* of Jesus Christ that is of importance here. Notice that in John 14, Jesus said "Whoever believes in me" will also do the works He has done. That is what it means to place full confidence in Jesus. Often when Jesus talked about faith, He coupled it with the opposite—lack of faith or doubt (e.g., Matthew 17:17, 20; 21:21) and Paul described Abraham as one who had "no unbelief," "fully convinced that God was able to do what He had promised" (Romans 4:20–21).

When Jesus rebuked His disciples for not being able to heal a boy, He said it was because of their "little faith" (Matthew 17:20). However, I don't believe Jesus was referring here to the size of their faith; I believe He was talking about their confidence. Other translations say "unbelief" or "lack of faith," and the word in the Greek comes from the word *oligopistos,* which means "lacking confidence." They weren't convinced God could do it. Jesus said that if they had faith the size of a mustard seed (which is tiny), they would be able to move mountains, so it's not so much the size of your faith that's important; what's important is fully believing Jesus is wholly able to do all things. Another way it could be put, as Saint Therese of Lisieux so eloquently put it, is "confidence in God's mercy."[10] After all, we are calling upon the mercy of God when we call out to Him in prayer.

Read Mark 10:46–52. What was it that enabled Bartimaeus to receive his sight? Bartimaeus *had confidence in God's mercy*. He stated what he wanted and was confident in Jesus's ability to respond. What is it you want Jesus to do for you today? You can boldly ask when your confidence is placed in who He is.

What seemingly impossible situation are you facing right now? Or if you aren't facing anything, think of someone else who is. Write it down. Ask the Lord to give you the faith in Him to believe He can change that situation and then bring it before Him in prayer. Keep praying persistently and record along the way how you see God answering your prayer.

*Ann's daughter Samuel
Chloe - Linda's Granddaughter*

[10] Manuscrits Autobiographiques, dedicated to Mother Mary of the Sacred Heart, Office Central de Lisieux, 1956, 237.

MATT. 18: 15-20 Dealing @ Sin in the Church
If brother/sister sins - keep between ↓.
If don't listen take 1 or 2 witnesses — NOT → church
NOT → pagan!

DAY
17

Corporate Prayer: Agreement

FILLED @ SPIRIT
SPEAK TRUTH BOLDLY

READ

Matthew 18:15-20
Acts 4:23-31; 12:5-17

BELIEVERS PRAYED

ACT. 4:23-31 Prayed together -
After praying, the place where they were
meeting was SHAKEN... then FILLED @ THE
HOLY SPIRIT & spoke the word of God BOLDLY.

12:5-17 Church earnestly prayed for Peter in prison
AN ANGEL APPEAR/JAIL LIT UP.... struck Peter
chains fell off - "Get up, QUICK."
Angel led him out of prison. Peter knocked on
Mary's home (MARK's MOTHER) Rhoda - PETER IS AT THE
DOOR. ASTONISHED! prayers were answered.

One of my favorite things to do on the planet is pray with others. There is nothing like hearing the heart of God for people and places and then coming together to agree that what we pray will be done. God is into family unity, and when His kids are all getting along, the sweetness of fellowship is exhilarating; after all, Jesus promised His presence when two or three are gathered in His name. I wonder if this is the reason why Matthew talked *FIRST* about making things right with a fellow believer who has wronged you before he talked about the power of *& THEN* coming together in prayer. After all, it's hard to agree with someone you're having a disagreement with.

The stories in Acts testify to the power of corporate prayer. In particular, the story of Peter being miraculously released from prison after the church gathered to pray earnestly for him is both powerful and humorous. We know the believers gathered together to pray rather than pray on their own because the word for church is literally "an assembly of people." Acts 12:12 says many were gathered together praying. We don't know how long they prayed for or how often, but they saw the importance of coming together to pray for their friend and brother in need. It is humorous that when their prayer was actually answered, they couldn't believe it—Peter was left outside the house knocking at the gate.

Maybe you're shy or an introvert, and you have a hard time being around groups of people. You might think, Can't I just pray on my own? The answer is yes and no. Yes, communing with God and interceding on your own is still necessary and powerful, but in a corporate gathering, you are saying, "I'm family, and I believe praying together in agreement makes a difference."

How have you viewed corporate prayer meetings in the past? Have they felt like a waste of time? Do you get bored? Does your mind start wandering when "that lady" starts praying a long, convoluted prayer? I encourage you to not give up. If your church prayer meetings seem dry, ask God to show you how to pray, and bring some fresh ideas to the leadership team. Get creative.

Do you have other like-minded young people you can pray together with? If not, reach out to a local youth pastor or youth leader, or a mentor, to talk to them about how you can gather to pray with other young people. You may like to start with just one friend. Be open to how the Lord will lead you to pray together with others.

I love my time @ my PRAYING SISTERS!

Ps. 41:13 Blessed be the Lord God of Israel
from everlasting → everlasting AMEN & AMEN

DAY
18

Do You
Need to Say
Amen?

READ

Psalm 41:13
Acts 1:12–14; 2:1–4
1 Corinthians 14:13–16

ACTS 1:12-14 All joined in prayer - MATTHIAS CHOSEN TO
REPLACE JUDAS.
2:1-4 Pentecost. All in one place - Soono - blowing VIOLENT WIND
came from HEAVEN - filled the house. Tongues of FIRE
resting of them! ALL - filled @ Holy Spirit
began to speak in other tongues as Spirit
enabled.

1 Cor. 14:13-16 The one who speaks in tongues should pray that
they may interpret what they say. Spirit prays - mind unfruitful.
PRAY @ SPIRIT - PRAY @ UNDERSTAND - I will sing @ understanding! -
How can someone say AMEN - if they don't know what you are saying.

As we have discussed, the early church valued corporate prayer. It's also what the direct disciples of Jesus did immediately after He ascended to heaven. It was in this climate of prayer that the promised Holy Spirit came. We don't have biblical evidence of what they were praying, but we know it was powerful. Did they say amen to the prayers of others, as we so often do in our corporate prayer gatherings? Is that why their prayers were answered? Why *do* we say amen at the end of a prayer? Is it just another one of those Christianese words that doesn't mean much?

Amen is a Hebrew word we can find in the Old Testament as well as the New Testament. In fact, it has been said it is the most well-known word in the world as it has remained unchanged from the original language.[11] Most often, it is used at the end of a discourse—a written or spoken communication—and when it is, it means "so it is," "so be it," or "may it be fulfilled." The *NAS New Testament Greek Lexicon* says "It was a custom, which passed over from the synagogues to the Christian assemblies, that when he who had read or discoursed, had offered up solemn prayer to God, the others responded Amen, and thus made the substance of what was uttered their own."[12]

We see Paul using the word a lot in his letters, especially at the end of a section giving glory to God or Christ, for example, in Ephesians 3:20–21, but

---

[11] "H543 - 'amen - Strong's Hebrew Lexicon (NIV)." *Blue Letter Bible*. www.blueletterbible.org. (Accessed 11 November, 2020.)

[12] Thayer, Joseph, *Thayer's Greek-English Lexicon of the New Testament,* (Hendrickson Publishers, 1996).

there are too many to list. This little word is a statement of affirmation that what we are praying is what we want to see done. We want to see God glorified, we want to see the prayers we pray together answered, we want to see God's kingdom come. There are other ways of expressing this like "I agree," or "Yes," or you might even hear someone say "Come on," but no matter the language, the heart behind it is the same. People who express this are passionate to see prayer fulfilled. *Amen.*

Have you been one to hold back in a corporate prayer gathering because you've been too afraid to express yourself? Even if you don't speak any prayers out loud, you can always be a part of it by saying "Amen" to others' words.

Next time you're in a corporate prayer gathering, ask God to give you the courage to pray something out loud. Don't be afraid of what may or may not come out of your mouth. Your confidence will build the more you do it. God is proud of you, no matter how it comes out.

You, Me, and Holy Spirit

I have been in so many corporate prayer gatherings that it's hard to pinpoint a standout. There have definitely been times when I haven't enjoyed praying corporately, but it is a very rare occasion. What makes it so fun to pray corporately? To sum it up: Holy Spirit. The Holy Spirit is in each believer present, and when we lay aside our own agenda and ask the Holy Spirit to lead and guide the prayer time, things happen. A flow begins from one prayer to another as He brings people, places, or situations to mind. One person might get a piece of the picture, another person another piece. Sometimes a holy fear will come upon the group and there is just silence as we stand or sit or lie in awe of our amazing God. Sometimes the Holy Spirit may lead us to pray for someone in the room and give them words of encouragement. Sometimes a song of worship will come forth. Sometimes the Holy Spirit may get someone to do something that seems unusual—for example, in 1949, revival in Argentina broke out because a woman felt led to bang a table with her hand during a prayer meeting. [13]

One of the most powerful experiences of corporate prayer in my life was when a group of us gathered in

---

[13] Miller, Edward R. *Secrets of the Argentine Revival.* (Peniel Publications, 1999).

Alice Springs, Australia, to pray. In the backyard of a humble home, Christians from different parts of Australia gathered—First Nations people and non-First Nations. As we prayed and worshiped, the glory of God was so strong that I had to fall to my hands and knees, and it took a lot of effort to move from that position after the prayer stopped as the weight of God's presence was so heavy. During another gathering, this time as we worshiped and prayed with a local congregation at a church, I had a prompting from the Lord to go up to the front to get the youth of the church to stand up and for us to pray for them. As a result of that act of obedience, something shifted in the spiritual atmosphere, and there was a freedom in worship and prayer that hadn't been there before.

Corporate prayer isn't just about getting together with other Christians. It's about getting together with them and God, and when we respond in obedience to His leadings, ground is taken for the kingdom.

Luke 2:25,26 — Simeon - righteous & devout. Waiting for consolation of Israel & Holy Spirit was on him. It was revealed by Holy Spirit he would not die until he had seen the Lord's Messiah.

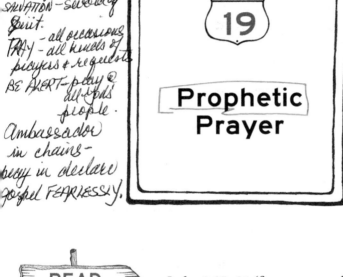

DAY
19

Prophetic Prayer

EPH. 6:17-20
Take up helmet of SALVATION - sword of Spirit.
PRAY - all occasions - all kinds of prayers & requests
BE ALERT - pray @ all God's people.
Ambassador in chains - pray in declare gospel FEARLESSLY.

READ — Luke 2:25–26 (for an example of how the Holy Spirit brings revelation)
Acts 9:1–20
Ephesians 6:17–20

ACTS 9:1-20 — Paul breathed murderous threats ag. Lord's disciples → Damascus to take men & women of the way to prison in Jerusalem.
Sudden light from heaven - FELL/HEARD voice.... "SAUL, SAUL WHY ARE YOU PERSECUTING ME." I am Jesus whom you are persecuting. Get up, go to city - you will be told what to do. Men w/ him heard a sound but saw NOTHING. Led him to Damascus. 3 DAYS blind - didn't eat or drink.
ANANIAS - vision - to house Judas - ask for Saul who is praying. In a vision he has seen a man # Ananias come / place his hands - RESTORE. ANANIAS feared Saul's reputation. GD - CHOSEN INSTRUMENT to proclaim Jesus → Gentiles. Ananias went - laid hands - PRAYED scales fell off - BAPTIZED. Saul spend several days in Damascus - preaching JESUS is the SON OF GOD!

As the previous story told, there is a connection between praying, listening, and obeying. While there can be differences of opinion on what prophetic prayer is, to me it is simply inclining our ear to God—seeking Him, listening to Him, and praying what comes into our heart and mind. In this instance, prophetic means "divine inspiration or revelation." We could call it inspired prayer.

Sometimes we don't even need to seek God to hear what to pray for. Often, He is the One who gets our attention and then it's an act of obedience for us to respond. Remember, God wants to share His secrets with His friends because He wants a love relationship with us (see day 10).

A good example of what this looks like in relation to intercession is a story from one of YFC Australia's main outreaches each year—Schoolies for Jesus. Schoolies is a massive event held in various locations around Australia. Thousands of school leavers—those who have just finished their final year of school—gather to party like there's no tomorrow. YFC sends teams of young people out on the streets to share the love of God with the Schoolies during this time. The teams always start with worship and prayer before they hit the streets. One particular night during this time, Rebecca[14] felt she shouldn't go out on the streets with the others as she normally would. Instead, she felt as if God was inviting her to stay back, find a quiet place, and pray for drug dealers. She spent the night obediently praying in this way while the others were on the streets sharing the

---

[14] Name changed for confidentiality.

gospel. When they returned to share what God did during that night, they said to Rebecca, "It was strange, but we kept on meeting people who were drug dealers and we were able to share the gospel with them."

While that may have come as a surprise to the young people evangelizing, it was no surprise to God and Rebecca—who had said a yes in her heart to the whisper of Jesus. There are many people out there who are just waiting for us to respond to the whispers of God in prayer. Will you be one to say yes?

REFLECT

Have you ever had a person, place, or situation come to mind and felt compelled to pray? How have you responded? Did you dismiss it as just a thought or were you moved to action? There is no need for condemnation if you missed it, but next time, consider what may happen if you're willing to say yes.

Pray for SLOAN at the Graduation Party!

Find a person you can practice praying with, whether it be a friend, youth leader or mentor. Tell them you want to practice prophetic prayer, i.e. listening to God and praying what He speaks to you. Begin your time together by just 'waiting' on God, that is by being still and silent, and asking Him to speak. You may pray something like this: "Lord, I want to pray what is on your heart, so please place on my heart what is on Yours." As something comes to mind, start praying together. Be open to other things He may place on your heart.

DAY 20

A Heavenly Vision

READ

Luke 1:22; 24:23
Acts 13:1-3
Revelation 5:8-14

*Zechariah made signs to them but could NOT speak. They realize he had seen a vision.

#1. Luke 1:22
#2. Luke 24:23 → The women at Jesus' tomb saw a vision of angel. Said Jesus was alive

Acts 13:1-3 while we worshipping & fasting Holy Spirit said; Set apart for me the Barnabas & Saul. They laid hands on them - sent them out!

Rev. 5:8-14 - Worshipping God - looked up - heard voice of many angels 1,000 or 1,000 10,000X Sang: Worthy is the Lamb..... Heard every creature... To Him who sits on the Throne & to the Lamb be PRAISE / HONOR / GLORY / POWER

Imagine putting yourself in the heavenly vision John shared as recorded in Revelation 5. Imagine you are one of the twenty-four elders, seeing the One who is worthy to take the scroll—the *only One* in heaven who is worthy, the Lamb who was slain but who has conquered all. What is your response? Of course, like the other elders, you want to bow down in worship before this One who is worthy. But as you bow, you have your harp in one hand and a golden bowl full of incense in the other. In the earthly sense, this seems extremely awkward. How can you bow down in awe when your hands are full? Because this One is worthy. When you realize what the harp and bowl symbolize, you want to offer it all to Him.

Throughout Revelation, the harp is symbolic of worship. Revelation 5; 14:2–3; and 15:2–3 all speak of people holding or playing harps, and when they do, a song emerges to the King. The golden bowls of incense are the prayers of the saints. What an amazing picture: the prayers of God's people, which include yours and mine, are presented before the One who is worthy. Doesn't it make you want to bow your knee right now and sing your praises to Him?

Worship and prayer are a natural fit. In beholding the One who is worthy, we can't help but let out heartfelt praise and present our prayers of thanksgiving. When we know that the One who has conquered all also wants to conquer our situations and circumstances, we are able to confidently present our requests to Him. Heartfelt worship and prayer also enable us to tune in to what the Holy Spirit wants us to do. For example, Acts 13:1–3 tells us that while the prophets and teachers of the church at Antioch were worshiping the Lord and fasting, the Holy Spirit gave them directions for what they were to do next.

Do you need a fresh word from the Lord? How about you worship the Lord for who He is right now and see what the Holy Spirit would like to say. But even if you don't sense Him saying anything, know that worshiping Him is enough because He is worthy.

How do you feel about singing? Do you absolutely love it or are you tone deaf? We are all different, but no matter how skilled or gifted you are, your voice makes a joyful melody to the Lord.

Put on some of your favorite worship music. Start worshiping and adoring the Lord. As you do so, see if any prayers of thanksgiving arise and pray them out to Him. Your worship time may turn into a time of intercession as the Lord places people and places on your heart. Be free to swing between worship in song and prayer. It all is a delight to the Lord.

DAY 21

What about the Lord's Prayer?

READ

Matthew 6:5–15; 14:23
Mark 1:35
Luke 5:15–16; 11:1–13; 18:9–14

What is known as the Lord's Prayer has to be one of the most well-known passages in the Bible. You probably have heard it recited, even if you have never read the Bible before, as it's used to open parliamentary proceedings in the Australian Government as well as on occasions such as weddings and funerals. Depending on what church you belong to, it may be recited weekly.

There are two places where it's recorded: in Matthew, as part of Jesus teaching His disciples in the Sermon on the Mount, and in Luke—a shortened version—in response to a disciple's question asking Him to teach them how to pray. The fact that one doesn't include all the words of the other indicates to me that it's not so much the exact words that are important but the meaning behind the words. Being Jews, the disciples would have known a certain way of praying, yet they noticed how frequently Jesus would draw aside to pray and wanted to know His way of praying.

I believe what Jesus said before the prayer is just as important (Matthew 6:5–8). Prayer isn't something you do to get the attention and praise of others; it is something between you and your heavenly Father. "Hallowed be your name" was Jesus highlighting how holy and set apart God is from any other being, and it's only His name that should be praised. When we pray "your kingdom come and your will be done," we are expressing a desire to see His rule and reign on the earth as it is in heaven. Then the prayer shifts to making requests for provision or personal needs. Jesus didn't need to ask for forgiveness of sin as He was perfect, yet it was important for His disciples to know forgiveness was found in God and that it needed to be extended to others.

God is looking for a humble heart that will honor Him first and foremost. Acknowledging how majestic and holy He is, and how worthy of praise above all other things, keeps our perspective clear and focuses our priorities in prayer. What a wonderful God we serve, and how worthy He is to receive all honor and glory and power.

Have you ever prayed this prayer out of habit or by rote? Or is it new to you?

Read through the Lord's prayer slowly, stopping after each verse. Contemplate on what it means for your life. You may like to pause and pray your own prayer after each verse. For example:

Lord's prayer: "Our Father in heaven, hallowed be your name."

Your prayer: Thank you that I can call you Father and that you are a good Father. I lift up your name above all other names and declare that you are holy and righteous. There is none like you.

Lord's prayer: "Your kingdom come and your will be done, on earth as it is in heaven."

Your prayer: Lord, there are many things on this earth that don't line up with your will. May you have your way in my heart first and foremost. May I live out your will for my life. May you reign and rule in my life and in this world.

Part 3

INCREASE

DAY 22

The Stone That Became a Mountain

Isaiah 9:1–7
Daniel 2:26–45
Matthew 4:12–17; 13:31–32
John 17:18–21

We have now arrived at the final part of our adventure. I know, how sad the adventure is nearing the end. Yet in reality, the adventure is just beginning. You see, knowing God and knowing how to commune with Him and pray for others is a key in His overall plan for history. We get to be a part of His big story in seeing the kingdom of God increase on the earth.

Jesus prayed for those who would believe as a result of the disciples sharing the Word. He knew that even though His time on earth was coming to an end, His work on the earth was not. It would continue through His chosen disciples. How exciting! Hundreds of years before Jesus came to the earth, the prophet Isaiah said One would come to bring a great light and the increase of His government and peace would know no end (Isaiah 9:1–7). Daniel, in interpreting King Nebuchadnezzar's dream, said the God of heaven would set up a kingdom that would never be destroyed. It would be like a stone cutting through all the earthly kingdoms and would grow to be a great mountain that filled the earth (Daniel 2:26–45). You and I are a part of this kingdom that has broken into the world through Jesus and will one day fill the entire earth.

The fact that this kingdom can never be shaken (Hebrews 12:28) is so reassuring as we go about the King's work in this world. When we hear of Christians being persecuted throughout the world each day; and of corrupt and ungodly governments ruling nations, wars, famines, and the like; we can feel like there is overwhelming defeat, but the reality is we cannot lose.

Throughout the next few days, we'll explore how you can partner with God through prayer to increase the kingdom of God "on earth as it is in heaven" (Matthew 6:10).

What is your view of the future of this world? Do you get disheartened as you watch the news and hear all the "bad" that is happening? When you hear God's promise that His kingdom will continue to increase and that it cannot be destroyed, how does that make you see things? Pray that you'll be able to see the world as God sees it.

Look into the history of the kingdoms that rose and fell as Daniel prophesied in Daniel 2. You may even see if you could draw the statue and find out the names of the kingdoms that came and went. Write down the names of the kingdoms next to the statue. If needed, get help from a youth leader or mentor.

I Have
the Power

READ

Matthew 28:18–20
Luke 9:1–2; 10:1–12, 17–24
John 13:1–17; 14:12
Colossians 2:9–10
1 John 4:17

On day 12, we explored the fact that we pray in the name of Jesus, and that this represents His power and authority to make things happen. It is so vital that we understand the authority we have in Him as we seek to see the kingdom of God increase around us. *All* authority has been given to Jesus, and because we are in Him, we have the same authority. Colossians 2:9–10 says the whole fullness of the Deity (God) dwells bodily in Christ, and we have been filled in Him, who is the head of all rule and authority. And 1 John 4:17 says as He is, so are we in this world. How amazing is that? So now, when we obey His command to go make disciples, we know we go with an indestructible power.

Just like the early followers of Jesus, it's in the act of obedience that we will see His authority demonstrated through us. We see in Luke 10 that as they obeyed Him in going out to the towns and villages to bring the kingdom of God, they rejoiced that demons were subject to them—Jesus had given them authority over *all* the power of the enemy (v. 19). This means they healed the sick (Luke 10:9) and cast out demons, demonstrating the kingdom of God was near. Jesus quickly reminded them that even though this was awesome, it's not what they were to focus on. They were to rejoice that their names were written in heaven, that is, they had a permanent home with Him.

One of the most remarkable acts of authority we see in the life of Jesus is found in John 13:3 which says Jesus, knowing the Father had given *all* things into His hands, washed His disciples' feet. He then told them to wash each other's feet. Having the authority of Jesus means we also humbly serve one another in love. How amazing and how different this looks compared to how the world views authority.

We get to partner with Jesus in increasing the kingdom of God through His authority in us by doing the same thing His early followers did. We can celebrate when we see His kingdom manifest, just as His disciples did, but let us not boast when we see the miraculous. Let us rejoice that we are His and will get to enjoy Him forever.

Have you ever thought it was possible for you to heal the sick or cast out demons, or have you thought it was only reserved for a special class of Christian? Meditate on the truth that because Jesus is in you, you have access to His authority. How does that make you feel?

Is there someone you know right now that is sick? Is there someone in need? Reach out to them and ask them if you could pray for them in person or go and do an act of service for someone in need, whether it be weeding their garden or cleaning their windows or something that you know would bless them.

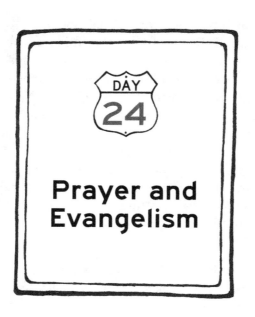

DAY 24

Prayer and Evangelism

READ

John 17:20–21
Acts 4:23–31
Romans 10:14–17
Colossians 4:2–6
2 Thessalonians 3:1–2

I think by now you have realized God is a supernatural God. He is all-powerful and is able to do anything. So why doesn't everyone know this amazing God? He could reveal Himself to every person on the earth and that would be it. No more evil, no more pain, no more sickness. That is a mystery we aren't going to have the answers for, but I do know that throughout the Bible, people are given a choice and God chooses to use people as the means by which He demonstrates His love and brings good news. As Paul said, "How beautiful are the feet of those who preach the good news" (Romans 10:15).

Evangelism is a word that isn't in the Bible, but it comes from the Greek word *evangelion* which *is* in the Bible and is translated as "gospel" (e.g., Mark 1:14–15 NASB), which is literally "good message." The good news of Jesus and His kingdom needs to be spread through people to see the increase we have spoken about, and prayer is a vital part of seeing this accomplished. From the passages you read today, there are three aspects to consider:

1. Praying for people who are intentionally preaching the gospel, especially in areas it's yet to have been preached in.

2. Praying for ourselves as we look for opportunities to share the gospel.

3. Praying for those who have not yet believed. We'll find out more about this in the coming days.

At the birth of the church in Jerusalem, heavy persecution came upon the believers who were preaching the Word of God, so they needed to pray for themselves to have the boldness to continue proclaiming it. God did the miraculous through them, but they still needed boldness to declare what the good message was, and many people were saved as a result. Paul requested prayer from the churches in Colossae and Thessalonica as he and his coworkers went from place to place to preach the Word of God. He wanted an open door so God's Word could be spread throughout the Roman Empire. Again, they were heavily persecuted for sharing, but the goodness of the gospel was too good to keep to themselves.

REFLECT

Are you encouraged by the faith and boldness of Jesus's early followers? What obstacles do you face in proclaiming the good news of the gospel? List them, and ask the Lord to give you the boldness to overcome.

ACT

Do you know anyone who has given their life to go and preach the good news to an unreached people group?

If not, research a mission organization for an area of the world you are interested in. Pray for the people who are reaching this part of the world.

DAY

25

Praying for Healing

READ

Psalm 103:3
Matthew 4:23–25; 10:1, 5–8
Luke 9:1–2; 10:9
Acts 2:42–43; 5:12–16

Did you know one of the names of God is *Jehovah Rapha* or "God who heals" (Exodus 15:26)? As Jesus is the exact image of God (see Hebrews 1:3 and Colossians 1:15), it then makes sense that Jesus came as a healer. Sickness and disease weren't in God's original design—everything He created was good (Genesis 1). When *Emmanuel,* "God with us," entered the scene of history, we see Him manifest healing to *all* who came to Him for healing. What a beautiful God we serve.

Every time we read about Jesus sending out His disciples, He commanded them to heal the sick. This was to display the kingdom of God was near. When He left to go back to heaven, the apostles continued His work of healing and teaching about the kingdom, and because of this, many thousands became followers.

As you are now in Christ, it is in your very nature to be a healer. Wow! The first time I prayed for healing for someone and it actually worked was at a youth camp. An older gentleman was complaining of a painful and swollen knee, which was hindering him in the service he came to do. During a prayer time, I felt prompted by the Holy Spirit to go and put my hand on his knee—after asking him if it was okay to do that— and to pray for healing. The pain left and the swelling went down. You could actually see the difference afterward. It was such a beautiful thing to see God's love for this man expressed through healing.

People have many questions about healing, and sometimes we don't see the results we want, but there is no doubt it is God's desire to heal, and we can be used by Him to bring that healing to others as we pray for them. I have seen many nonbelievers begin to soften when they have been healed after someone prayed for them. When the first disciples went out to bring the kingdom to others, some people didn't receive them, and it will be the same for us as we step out to pray for others. They just moved on when that happened, and so should we. But if we are willing to obey Jesus when He prompts us, we will be His agents of increase in this world.

What is it that motivates us to heal the sick? Yes, we want to see God's kingdom increase and people come to believe in Him, but if we look at Jesus, the thing that motivated Him was compassion.

Look up the number of times in the gospels Jesus was moved by compassion to heal. Write the chapter and verse and what He did.

STORY FROM LIFE

Freedom to Dance: A Miracle Story

Early in 2019, Franklin Graham, the son of the well-known evangelist Billy Graham, came to share the gospel in the city I was living in. The Billy Graham Evangelistic Association hired out the convention center, and it was packed to capacity.

When the call was given for people to surrender their lives to Jesus, hundreds went down to the front, including a certain Aboriginal lady and her daughter. I was one of the prayer volunteers at the event and talked to this lady to find out if she had ever received Christ before. After digging a little deeper, I found out she was already a Christian but her sister had wanted to come down to the front but couldn't due to a problem with her legs. I said I would go with her to her sister.

She was right up at the back of the auditorium, and I led her through the prayer to give her life to Christ. I then asked if I could pray for her legs. She said yes, and when I did, I asked her to get up and test it out. She got up and all pain had left. I asked her to do something she couldn't do before prayer—to start dancing, and so she started dancing then and there with a big smile on her face.

A teenage member of their family then asked for prayer. I explained that because this lady now had Christ in her, she could pray for the young man. I guided her in what to do and how to pray, and this young man's back was also freed from pain. This goes to show that it doesn't matter how long you've been born again; with Christ in you, you can do the miraculous.

DAY
26

Supernatural Insight

READ

John 1:45–50
Acts 2:14–18; 10:1–3
1 Corinthians 12:1–11
2 Corinthians 12:1–4

"Are you having nightmares?" That's the question I asked a teenager I had only just met during a visit to a local youth detention center.

"How did you know?" he responded with somewhat defensive interest.

I was hanging out and chatting with a group of teenagers in the detention center, and while I talked with them, I was also talking with God to see if there was anything He wanted to bring up or encourage them with.

I knew I had to speak with this young man in particular. On the outside he seemed rough and tough, but that initial prayer—of simply asking God what I should start the conversation with—led to an in-depth discussion about God and how to have a relationship with Him. I was also able to pray the nightmares would leave.

The question asked was from a word of knowledge God had given me. It came to me in one single word in my mind—"nightmares." Sometimes people may get a picture in their mind to know what is happening in a person's life, or an impression in their spirit, or even a pain in their body to indicate a person is feeling pain. However the "knowledge" comes, it is a supernatural knowing or revelation from God. Paul talked about many visions and revelations he received from God. Throughout the book of Acts, we see God speaking in supernatural ways to people to give them insight they would otherwise not have, for the purpose of expanding the kingdom.

As we have already explored, God desires to speak to His children, and if we ask Him as we take steps to introduce people to God, He will give us insight to help us along the way. Sometimes we may think we have a special revelation for someone but it is wrong. Or maybe we are right but they are too afraid to admit it. In such instances we can simply say we are learning to hear God's voice and we thought that's what He said. Despite what happens, we need to make sure we are demonstrating God's love. If we never take a risk because we are afraid of getting it wrong, then we may just miss out on the blessing of being able to introduce someone to this supernatural God.

What do you think when you read that you may be able to receive information from God about someone you wouldn't know otherwise? God shares His secrets with His friends.

Do you desire to grow in this area? Reach out to your youth pastor/leader or mentor and ask them to help you connect with others who also may be wanting to grow in this area. Perhaps there is a course you can take at a local church or further reading you can do.

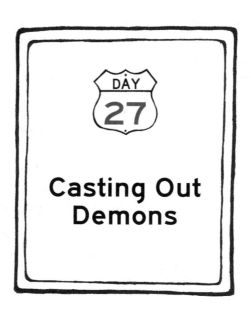

DAY 27

Casting Out Demons

READ

Matthew 7:21–22
Mark 3:13–15; 16:15–20
Acts 16:18; 19:11–20
Ephesians 6:10–12

Can you place yourself in the chapters of the Gospels and imagine you are part of the crowd following Jesus? It must have been absolutely chaotic at times, but you can't keep your eyes off this Jesus who is so full of love and compassion for those who are suffering yet so full of power and authority. You are amazed that by one word, a person who has been tormented by evil spirits for years is completely set free.

Then Jesus calls you to be one of His chosen ones. You are thrilled, but when He gives you the authority to do exactly as He has been doing, you aren't quite sure if you're made of the right stuff. *Can I actually do this? What if I screw up?* You remember His words: "These signs will accompany those who believe: In my name they will cast out demons" (Mark 16:17). *Oh, that's right, all I have to do is believe. It's Jesus's power and authority, it's His name I carry, and that will accomplish the work. He promised to never leave me or forsake me.*

Can you identify with the early disciples in their doubts and insecurities? I sure can. We don't often like to talk about the reality of demons in our church gatherings. Often when we do, it can be fear inducing, and we feel ill-equipped to deal with anything that's going on in the unseen realm. But it's undeniable from the biblical account that the demonic is something that is real and going on in the world today. Ephesians 6 says our struggle is not against flesh and blood but "against the spiritual forces of wickedness in the heavenly places" (v. 12 NASB). But the good news is that as Christians, we don't need to be afraid of evil spirits. When we know who we are in Christ and who He is in us, we know we have the power and authority to deal with them. In fact, we can see people totally set free too.

When Jesus recognized demons working in someone, or they recognized Him, He simply commanded them to get out. We can get caught up in methods of what to say or what not to say, what to do or what not to do, and read theology around whether people are oppressed or possessed, but I don't think this is very helpful. All I know is demons stink, they are stopping people from encountering the freedom Jesus purchased for them, and we have the authority to do something about it. The biggest weapon against the demonic is intimacy with Jesus. When you know Him, the demons will know you and will flee at His name. So don't go out trying to look for demons, but pursue Jesus, and when you do come across one, you and Jesus can deal with it together.

How do you feel about the reality of evil spirits? Is it something that freaks you out or something you have experienced? Meditate on the fact that Jesus is the victorious One who resides in you. Wait upon the Lord and ask Him how He sees demons. What did He say?

The spiritual realm is very real and sometimes we have opened spiritual doorways for the enemy to enter our lives through activities we have been involved in or even things we may have watched on TV or over the internet. If you feel like you are being oppressed by any evil spirit, say sorry to God for anything you may have done to open the doorway and reach out to a youth pastor or leader to ask for help.

A Captive Set Free

I have a good friend in Canada who loves to pray for people out on the streets. God does a lot of wonderful things through him, and this story comes from him.

I was visiting some good friends of mine in Redding, California. They lived and ministered in an area that was known for drugs and crime. One evening, we were out on the streets ministering when we came across a fellow who had had a little too much to drink. He was a friendly drunk, and when he heard we were Christians, he said he knew a Christian song and he started singing "Amazing Grace." We gladly joined in. As we prayed for him, he began to sober up and we were able to share the gospel with him.

But all of a sudden, things began to change and he became angry and aggressive. We knew we were dealing with something spiritual. A demon had taken over and was causing him to be this way. The friend I was with simply said we wanted to talk to Dave,[15] and we were able to invite him over to the apartment where we were staying.

We shared the love of Jesus and the good news of the gospel, and in the apartment that night, another one of God's precious sons came into the kingdom as he

---

[15] Name changed for confidentiality.

surrendered his life to Jesus. As a result, Dave was totally set free from an evil spirit.

It is so fun seeing people set free from the grip of the enemy and become all they were created to be. God is just looking for willing vessels to say yes. Will you be one of those who says yes to increasing the kingdom?

DAY
28

The Tangible
Presence of
the Holy Spirit

READ

John 16:7
Acts 2:1–12
Romans 14:17
Galatians 5:22–23

One Easter, I traveled to a beautiful national park for a break. Along the way, I decided to stop in a little town to buy some chocolate Easter eggs. Sitting outside the front of the shops was a group of local young people, so I engaged in conversation with them. I gave them some Easter eggs and I asked if they knew what Easter was about. To my surprise, most of them didn't know, so I shared the Easter story with them. I then asked them if they had heard of the Holy Spirit. One girl said she had gone to a school called Holy Spirit in another state. Other than that, they didn't have any grid for Him. I asked if any of them would like to feel the Holy Spirit, as He is real and active. A couple of them did, so I got them to place out their hands and prayed a simple prayer inviting the Holy Spirit to come and make Himself known to these young people. Both of the young people felt a warmth and peace they hadn't felt before and were very curious. I was able to explain to them how much God loves them and was doing this to show them that His love, warmth, and peace could be theirs forever. While none of these young people surrendered their lives to Jesus that day, a seed was planted that another person could come and water.

Paul tells us the kingdom of God is a matter of righteousness, peace, and joy in the Holy Spirit. This doesn't just *look* like something in a believer's life, it often *feels* like something. When the Holy Spirit was first poured out on the believers at Pentecost, the surrounding people thought they were drunk. The believers actually seemed intoxicated because of the gift of tongues poured out through them, and I'm sure the joy was manifest too. Because the Holy

Spirit is pursuing people, when we pray for people who don't yet know Him, they will often feel things they have never experienced before such as warmth, a refreshment, overwhelming peace, or joy. There have been many occasions when I have prayed for people on the street and this has happened but I don't actually feel it myself. Jesus knows the people we are praying for and knows what experience of Him they need, so we just leave the results to Him; and when it happens, a door is opened for the gospel to be preached. Let's not be afraid of allowing the Holy Spirit to make Himself known. He is as much God as the Father and the Son.

Have you ever had an experience where you felt something was outside of your normal feelings? How did you react? Is there a gift from the Holy Spirit you desire to experience that you haven't before? Ask Him for that gift.

The fruit of the Spirit is love, joy, peace, patience, kindness, goodness, faithfulness, gentleness and self-control (Galatians 5:22-23), and when you have Him, these are the things that should manifest in your life. If they aren't, ask the Holy Spirit to reveal what is stopping that. Put into action anything He tells you to do.

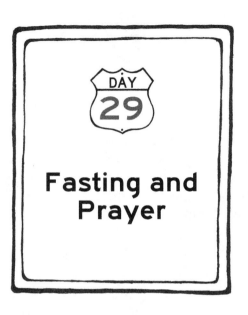

DAY 29

Fasting and Prayer

READ

Matthew 6:16–18; 9:14–17
Luke 4:1–14
Acts 10:30–31; 13:1–3

I heard a pretty cool story when I spent three months in Canada in 2019. A Youth for Christ chapter in Central Alberta desperately wanted to see young people come to know Jesus. Seven of the staff felt led to fast and pray for a week for twelve young people in their community to give their lives to Jesus. Not long after this week, they ran an outreach event and invited the young people to put their trust in Jesus. And guess how many young people responded? Yes, twelve. Now was that just a coincidence or is there a correlation between fasting and prayer and seeing answers?

Fasting is simply abstaining from food or certain types of foods, and sometimes drink, for a specified amount of time. Fasting was a normal part of life for a Jew, mainly on the Day of Atonement (see Leviticus 16:29–31), but at other times, fasts were done to mourn or show deep repentance (e.g., 1 Chronicles 10:8–12; Daniel 9:3). In modern times, we may fast from other things we have an attachment to, for example, our phone, TV, social media, or video games.

In the time of Jesus, different groups, such as the Pharisees, fasted religiously, and they were curious as to why Jesus's followers did not fast. Jesus's response indicated He was ushering in a new way. He shared how in a Jewish wedding feast, a massive celebration goes on for seven days and is free to all those who come, paid for by the bridegroom's family.[16] Jesus is the bridegroom, and He was with

---

[16] Green, M. *The Message of Matthew (The Bible Speaks Today Commentary).* (Leicester, England, Intervarsity Press, 2000), 125.

His disciples so there was much rejoicing and celebration, but there would be a time for fasting when He was no longer with them (Matthew 9:15). His parable about not using a piece of new cloth to patch an old garment and not putting new wine in old wineskins (Mark 2:21–22) meant His way wasn't going to be like the Jewish religious system. The new way was incompatible with the old. So while we don't see specific incidences of the disciples of Jesus fasting, we do see it in Acts once Jesus had departed.

In the Christian life, there are no specific stipulations or obligations to fast, but at certain times we can fast to be solely focused on time with the Lord and prayer. This act of self-discipline shows we mean business with God,[17] and if done with the right heart motive, brings reward (Matthew 6:16–18). Is that reward answered prayer? Is that reward being more in tune with God's voice (Acts 13:2)? Is that reward being empowered by the Spirit (Luke 4:14)? Stories like the one from Canada would indicate it very well could be all of those things.

Have you ever tried fasting? What was it like? The appetite for food is one of the strongest desires in a

---

[17] Ibid., 102.

human, but eating can be resisted for a period of time without harm, other than some bad hunger pains. If you feel the Lord asking you to do a fast, ask Him for how long. If you plan to do an extended fast, you should make sure you have the knowledge of how to begin and end properly.

For some practical guidelines, look up '7 Basic Steps to Successful Fasting and Prayer' by Dr Bill Bright,[18] but please make sure you consult a doctor for guidance if in doubt and if you have any medical conditions. If you are under eighteen, I would also recommend getting the blessing of your parents and listening to them if they have concerns.

For more advice and guidelines on fasting, see the YFCI fasting guidelines link in the footnotes.[19]

ACT

If you don't have any medical conditions that would limit you, try a one day fast. Write about your experience afterwards. What did God speak to you during this time? If you are under 18, please ask your parents about it first.

---

[18] https://www.cru.org/us/en/train-and-grow/spiritual-growth/fasting/7-steps-to-fasting.html
[19] Adam Shepski, "YFCI Fasting Guidelines." Posted January, 2017. *Youth for Christ International.* www.yfci.org. PDF.

DAY
30

What If My
Prayer
Doesn't Work?

READ

Matthew 17:14–20
Mark 9:14–29
John 4:33–38
1 Corinthians 3:4–9

I have already touched on perseverance in prayer when interceding for someone or something (day 14) but what if, when we step out to pray for someone directly, we don't see a result immediately? The disciples of Jesus had this seemingly embarrassing situation happen to them. They couldn't cast out a demon from a young boy when his father asked them to. They had already been given authority by Jesus to cast out demons (Mark 3:15), so why didn't it happen this time?

Jesus rebuked them for their lack of faith. I talked about faith on day 16 as an important aspect of prayer. I can almost sense Jesus's thoughts—*Come on, guys, I gave you authority. Don't you believe in the authority I have given you?* As you saw, it didn't matter about the size of the faith; it was *who* faith was put in that mattered. But I wonder if here, when Jesus said this type could only come out through prayer, He was indicating the kind of prayer they needed was the one prayed in secret, where someone communed with Him and where God could remind them of the authority they actually had? What if the kind of faith they needed was faith in the authority Jesus had given them? This, of course, is speculation but worth consideration. Some manuscripts of the Bible say it required prayer *and* fasting. Whether fasting is required as well or not, the fact that fasting helps us be intentional in our relationship with God— which reminds us of who He is and who we are in Him—is what matters.

If we are disappointed in not seeing prayer answered, we could ask ourselves a few questions. Do I have faith in Jesus? Do I believe He is the God of the impossible? Do I believe I have the authority of Jesus within me? Am I fellowshiping with God in prayer? Ultimately, if we can say yes to these things, when we pray for someone and don't see it "work," we have to trust God with the outcome. I have heard numerous stories where people have prayed for someone and they haven't seen a change immediately, yet afterward they have heard the person woke up different the next day. Or a seed was sown in a person's life because a believer stepped out to pray for someone, and when another believer came along and watered this seed, they reaped the harvest of what the other person had sown. As Paul encouraged the Galatians, I encourage you, "Let us not become weary in doing good, for at the proper time we will reap a harvest if we do not give up" (Galatians 6:9).

What has your attitude been when you don't see prayer answered when you've stepped out, believing God would have you pray for someone? I believe God would be so proud of you for simply being obedient and taking a risk. Don't let disappointments rob you of the joy of being part of increasing God's kingdom.

Heidi Baker works among the poorest of the poor in Mozambique. She prayed for many blind people before she saw her first healing of blind eyes. Watch the video of her story—the link is in the footnotes. Write down some things that stood out to you as you watched.[20]

---

[20] "Heidi Baker Prays for Blind People." Posted January 2, 2016. *God Talk.*
https://www.youtube.com/watch?v=ftYjWFOquHA. (Accessed November 11, 2020.)

DAY
31

What Now?

READ

John 17
Hebrews 12:1–2

We have come to the end of our thirty-one-day adventure on prayer. In the beginning, it was stated that the desire was to see you incorporate prayer into your daily life. I hope by now you are beginning to enjoy a deep sense of intimacy with your Father, you are hearing His voice, and you are learning to walk in obedience. I also hope you have gained a greater desire to intercede for those around you and for the issues in our world, and you are seeing your role in the bigger picture of increasing the kingdom.

As we began, we finish with John 17, this beautiful prayer of Jesus. Let's draw some final encouragement from this passage, knowing this isn't the end of the adventure of a life with God but a continuing journey.

1. Firstly, glorify God by being obedient to Him (v. 4). In *The Passion Translation,* it says Jesus glorified the Father by faithfully doing everything He told Him to do. You bring great glory to God by being obedient to His voice.

2. Secondly, keep an eternal perspective (vv. 14–16). When people give you a hard time because of what you stand for, or even hate you because of your allegiance to Jesus, remember that just as Jesus didn't belong to this world, you don't either. You belong to an eternal kingdom that will never fade away.

3. Thirdly, cling to truth (v. 17). God's Word is truth, and in this day of relative truth, this is not a popular statement. Holding on to the

truth of God's Word will give you a compass for your entire life.

4. Fourthly, maintain unity with God and fellow believers (vv. 21–23). This is a significant witness to the world. People will see you are Jesus's disciple if you love your brothers and sisters in Christ well, whether you agree fully with them or not (John 13:34–35).

5. Lastly, may you know and experience the endless love of the Father, just as Jesus did (v. 26). If you stay plugged in to the love of God, you will be sustained throughout your life as this is the kind of love that is truly satisfying. You could be in the toughest of situations, but if you truly know the love of God, you will be able to persevere.

I'm excited for you as you embark on your lifelong adventure with Jesus. May you run the race He has set out for you with perseverance, and may you know the delight of His heart for you. Go forth, young man, young woman, with great confidence in knowing who you are as a beloved son, as a beloved daughter.

What are the things that have stood out to you during the past thirty-one days? Take some time to record the things you have learned the most or that you have been challenged by the most. If you have been journeying with a youth leader or mentor, share these things with them.

What is the next step of obedience for you to take? Spend some time seeking the Lord and ask Him the question "What now?". Write down what He says. I pray you'll have the courage to take that step and see what God unfolds for you! Again, if you have a youth leader or mentor you trust, I encourage you to share this with them for mutual encouragement and accountability.

And finally, if this book has made a difference in your life, ask God if there is someone He wants you to pass this book onto, and be willing to become an encourager or mentor to them as they go through it.

About the Author

Lyndal J Walker is the international prayer director for Youth for Christ International. She has had a passion for prayer ever since seeing the *Transformations* videos as a young adult, desiring to see transformation of whole communities through the gospel. For ten years she lived and worked in the Top End of the Northern Territory, Australia, mainly with First Nations youth in a variety of capacities, including chaplaincy, teaching, house parenting, and prison ministry. In 2016, Lyndal completed her masters of education researching the perspectives on education of disengaged First Nations youth.

She worked as the National Prayer Coordinator for Youth for Christ Australia (YFCA) for two and a half years before transitioning to the international role. Her journey with YFCA began in 2015 with a desire to see young people walking in their true identity in Christ and living a life of intimacy with Him. She believes young people can become lifelong disciples of Jesus, living in the freedom and power of the gospel and bringing the kingdom "on earth as it is in heaven."

Lyndal travels the world to train and equip people in intimacy, intercession, and prayer evangelism, and she releases the prophetic to encourage the body of Christ to be all God created it to be.

Contact Lyndal

Email: lyndal.walker@yfci.org

More about YFC

Youth for Christ International is a Christian interdenominational, nonprofit, evangelical youth movement operating in over 110 countries. At its core, YFC is a movement of people unified by a common heart for sharing the good news of Jesus with young people in ways that are relevant to them in the context of their culture and life circumstances.

It is our desire for all young people to encounter Jesus, to experience radical freedom, and to truly understand their identity as sons and daughters of God.

YFCI: www.yfci.org

Free leaders supplement also available at lyndaljwalker.com and yfci.org

Acknowledgments

To Father, Son, and Holy Spirit, thank you for being my everything and for teaching me how to be.

To my family, Bev and Terry Walker and Kylie and Mandy, for enabling me to do what I do.

To my First Nations family and Christian leaders—who have taught me much about prayer and who have faithfully stood in the midst of much hardship. You are inspirational.

To my good friends who have been with me through thick and thin over many years and who have believed in me when I haven't believed in myself. You know who you are.

To my prayer team—thank you for being willing to stand in the gap on my behalf. I'm sure I'm only still standing because of your faithfulness in prayer.

To my financial supporters—you're the reason I can keep eating, sleeping, driving, traveling, etc., etc. I so value you.

To my YFC Australia family—thanks for cheering me on and teaching me so much about ministry, especially David and Ruth Ridley, who I first worked with in the Northern Territory; and for Cindy McGarvie, for believing in my gifting and giving me the opportunity to fly. And to all the young workers and volunteers I've worked with—for allowing me to be myself in your presence (we won't tell them all the silly things we've done together), and for your radical obedience to King Jesus.

To YFC International and Dave Brereton—for saying yes to this unknown Aussie and for entrusting me with this worldwide family. What a privilege!

To Warwick Vincent, Sue Tinworth, and Glenn Duncan for doing the first read-through and giving valuable feedback and encouragement. You are such warriors in the spirit whom I greatly admire.

Thanks, Sally, for guiding me in this process as a first-time book author.

Journal

Paul Craig – ♡
Sammie, Ann's daughter – CANCER
Keri ✳ biopsy
Lawrence – cancer
Partner – Ali, Paul M, Kaitlyn, Matt
Lise –
Chloe –
Dena –
Morrison Family

"Jets" 705 - 718 - 3376

Dark Spots ⇒ RED GRAPES
BLUE BERRIES

Polyphenol Dark spot diminisher

"Dr. Zelzel"

Chloe
Sammy
Lisa

2 chick. Breast milk
2 large pot. salt/pep/p day.
potatoes/onions (BOTTOM)
Chicken / salt / pep.
2 eggs bcz. Yogurt
tomatoes/cheese
parsley.

9 781736 503904